P9-ELO-764

Rebecca Donnelly

REBECCA DONNELLY

THE FRIENDSHIP LIE

CAPSTONE EDITIONS
a capstone imprint

The Friendship Lie is published by Capstone Editions,
a Capstone imprint
1710 Roe Crest Drive
North Mankato, Minnesota 56003
www.mycapstone.com

Library of Congress Cataloging-in-Publication Data
Names: Donnelly, Rebecca, author.
Title: The friendship lie / by Rebecca Donnelly.
Description: North Mankato, Minnesota : Capstone Editions, [2019] |
Summary:
Fifth-grader Cora feels her life is like the garbage her scientist-parents track, as their marriage is ending and Cora's best friend, Sybella, has thrown her away for a new girl.
Identifiers: LCCN 2018050333| ISBN 9781684460618 (hardcover) | ISBN 9781684460625 (ebook pdf)
Subjects: | CYAC: Friendship—Fiction. | Brothers and sisters—Fiction. | Twins—Fiction. | Refuse and refuse disposal—Fiction. | Recycling (Waste)—Fiction. | Family problems—Fiction. | Diaries—Fiction.
Classification: LCC PZ7.1.D65 Fri 2019 | DDC [Fic]—dc23
LC record available at https://lccn.loc.gov/2018050333

Design Elements: Shutterstock: Arizzona Design, fim.design, My Life Graphic

Cover illustration by Ramona Kaulitzki
Design by Hilary Wacholz

Printed and bound in China.
1671

For Molly,
with gratitude

Cora

Now

Cora Davis's life jacket smelled like fish. Probably a hundred kids had worn it on a hundred expeditions on the bay. Probably they had held a lot of fish while they were wearing it. She wanted to take it off, but that would be violating Boat Rule #1: Life jacket goes on and stays on. Even if you were in the classroom of the *Alleen B*, not out on deck, you kept your life jacket on. The marine science instructors, a couple of athletic-looking college students named Jilly and Jen, had made that very clear.

Cora wanted to say that she didn't need a life jacket because she shouldn't have been on the boat in the first place. She knew how to swim. She could jump overboard and make it back to land on her own.

But if Cora wasn't supposed to be there, on a fish data expedition on the San Francisco Bay with Sybella, the one person she was hoping, sort of, maybe, to avoid forever, where was she supposed to be? She had no idea.

She could see directly out to where Sybella was working. Sybella looked perfectly at home, but Cora felt lost.

Sybella was helping to haul a long, green net out of the water. She gripped the net while Jilly and Jen pulled it on board and set it in the open touch tank, where the fish waited to be counted, measured, and identified before going back into the bay. Cora watched from inside the glass-walled classroom as fish slipped and slopped out of the net and water splashed on the rubber deck of the *Alleen B.*

Sybella startled as a long, gray fish slid out of her hands. It splashed back into the touch tank, but Cora imagined that instead, it had leaped into the air, past the outstretched arms of Sybella and Jilly and Jen, over the side of the boat, and back into the water, free. She imagined she was that fish. She would belly-flop into the bay and swim as far as she could from the boat and from Sybella, who had once been her best friend and was not her best friend anymore.

Kyle should have been there. As Cora's twin, he

should have known she would be nervous about being stuck on a boat with Sybella, after everything that had happened. Twins were good at knowing things like that, and Kyle had been the best twin all eleven years of their lives.

He should also have known that Cora didn't belong there. It was his masterpiece at the art contest and his performance in the Trashlympics that had tied for first place with Sybella and won this so-called grand prize. Cora hadn't earned anything. You shouldn't be able to transfer prizes to other people, especially if the prize was something the other person didn't want.

But their dad had agreed to the switch because it was educational and Cora needed more educational opportunities. Kyle was visiting Sir Walter Dog at the Humane Society as part of his fifth-grade service learning project, and Cora was sitting by herself on this very educational adventure, staring at a poster that showed you how to measure a fish.

Jilly stuck her head into the classroom and said, "Come on out! I thought you were supposed to be super excited about this trip. Didn't you win it in a recycling contest or something?"

"Sybella did," said Cora. "I'm just here because . . . I don't know why I'm here. My dad made me come."

"Well, you're missing out," said Jilly. "Your friend

just caught a sixgill shark. And anyway, it's almost time for lunch. Let's go."

Friend. Cora let that word wash over her. She felt like she'd swallowed seawater.

Cora

Before

DR. CLARE WILSON'S VOICEMAIL

Twin Phone

"Please listen to this very important public service announcement. What is sustainability? *Sustainability* means thinking about the future and trying really hard to make sure that the things you have now, all the things you need, are going to be there in the future. Because sometimes they can go away, even when you're not expecting it. Sometimes you really need them, and they're just not there."

Speaker　　Call Back　　Delete

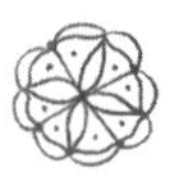

Cora and Sybella met on the first day of second grade. Sybella and her parents had moved from Wisconsin at the end of the summer, and Sybella hadn't met anyone her own age yet. Cora had always known one person her own age—Kyle—but she didn't have any other close friends. When you had a twin, you always had someone close by. She hadn't known she'd needed another friend until Sybella arrived.

When Sybella stood shyly in the classroom doorway on that first day, wearing a puffy coat that went almost to her ankles, the hood cinched tight around her pretty brown face, Cora knew that she and Sybella just went together. She couldn't explain how she knew that. It was a little like how she and Kyle just went together.

One of the other kids asked, not very nicely, why Sybella was wearing a winter coat in August, in California of all places. Sybella explained that she was on an expedition to the frozen North, but she'd gotten a little lost. Cora saw that Sybella was an adventurer, which was a good sign.

There were other good signs too: They had the same birthday, which was like being triplets instead of twins. And their parents all worked at UC Berkeley, although in different departments. Sybella's parents were chemical engineers, and Cora and Kyle's were in the environmental science department.

Their dad ran a garbology project that studied what happened to people's trash and recycling after they put it all in their curbside bins. Their mother worked on the technology that tracked each lucky piece of garbage that was part of the project. Sometimes they saw Sybella on campus, and once they played tag while their parents all chatted together about the school garden program. Basically, they *had* to be friends.

Cora was so sure of this that she decided to let Sybella in on the biggest secret of her life.

One day early in September of second grade, Sybella hung her long coat on the chain-link fence and climbed to the top of the playground bars. "I declare these bars in the name of . . . " She paused. "In the name of . . ."

"Room One-Twelve?" said Olla.

"Nope."

"Marshall Elementary?" said Wara.

"Not that either."

Olla and Wara drifted away, and Cora climbed halfway up the bars. She stretched herself as far as she could and whispered, "Aquafaba?"

Sybella leaned over, looking interested. "What?"

"Aquafaba," Cora repeated a little louder, but not so loud that anyone else could hear. She and Kyle were the only two who knew about Aquafaba, unless you counted Dr. Davis and Dr. Davis, their parents, who were very clever but not very imaginative, and liked to teach but didn't like to play.

"Where's that?" asked Sybella, as if she already knew that it was a *where* instead of a *what*. As if she could sense that an adventure was about to happen.

Cora knew that telling her had been the right choice.

"It's everywhere," she said. "Anywhere."

In first grade, Cora had found the word *aquafaba* in a dairy-free cookbook, and as soon as she'd whispered it to herself, she knew what it meant. Aquafaba was not just the liquid that came from a can of chickpeas, it was an entire watery world, a place for mer-children, mer-twins, where there were no arguing parents, no unhappy dinners, and no garbage.

Cora's parents worked with garbage all day, and they talked a lot about garbage at home too. They agreed on the problems, but sometimes they argued over the solutions, and then they argued over other things as well.

Cora knew that it was all very important. She had been told many times that the fate of the planet depended partly on what people decided to do with their trash. But sometimes she needed to be somewhere different, where no one went through her garbage can to see what she might have thrown away that week, and no one marked each candy wrapper on a chart in the living room for the whole family to see and discuss.

"I'll go," said Sybella. "How do we get there? Do we close our eyes? Wiggle our noses? Do we go on a boat?"

"No," said Cora. "We're already there. See?"

She pointed down at the ground and up at the clouds, and at the slide, the swings, and the spinning mushroom that made you want to throw up.

"I see," said Sybella. They jumped down from the bars and began to explore. Kyle was out sick, so they had Aquafaba to themselves. "I think."

Cora wanted to explain it all to Sybella, the whole history and geography and even the *smell* of Aquafaba, but it was hard to put into words. It was underwater, but it wasn't. It was a place you could go, if you thought of your feelings as a place, but there was no map showing how to get there.

They used their imaginations in Aquafaba, but *imaginary* didn't sound right. They pretended things all the time, but Aquafaba didn't feel pretend.

"So it's the same as here, but it's different?" said Sybella when Cora finished talking.

"Exactly!" That was a perfect description of Aquafaba. It was a glimmer overlaid on the real world, like a fancy scarf spread out on top of a dresser. All you had to do was use its name, and everything became magical.

"What are the rules?" asked Sybella when they were balancing on the toeholds of the outdoor climbing wall.

Cora shrugged. "No rules," she said. "Except we have different words sometimes."

Mer-twins with their own kingdom needed a language to go along with it, but Cora and Kyle had been too busy playing to make up an entire language. They settled for code words instead. That had been Kyle's idea. He came up with a long list of code words for animals, but Cora didn't talk much about animals, so he mostly used those himself. *Brussels sprouts,* meaning "candy," was one of Cora's favorites. They could say to each other, "Do you have any brussels sprouts?" Or,

"Brussels sprouts in Aquafaba!" And their parents would be clueless.

Sybella threw herself into the game. She was a natural mer-kid, and she'd even brought a pair of sunglasses with clamshell frames in sparkly blue and green that she let Cora wear too. Sybella was exactly what Aquafaba needed: someone brave enough to explore the North Pole. Someone brave enough to dress like an Arctic explorer in August in California.

Kyle came back to school the next day, and the game continued. They taught Sybella all their words, like *bamboozle* (soda) and *Alcatraz* (gum). Sybella was the one to suggest that they needed a motto, and she thought they should use Latin, because everything serious, like scientific names, came in Latin. *Aquafaba patria est:* "Aquafaba is my country." Or "a country," or something like that, according to the translator website. But it didn't really matter, because it wasn't just Latin, it was Aquafabian Latin, so it meant exactly what they wanted it to mean.

They played Aquafaba through all of second grade, and through third and fourth. Then they found themselves standing on the edge of fifth grade, like people looking down from a cliff at the edge of the ocean. They knew where they were now, but this was their last year at Thurgood Marshall Elementary, and after that, who knew? Sixth grade—middle school—was another continent.

"Fifth grade," said Sybella, as they walked through the gate on the first day. "Fifth. Grade."

"Fifth grade!" said Kyle, dancing around Cora and Sybella, his backpack bouncing up and down on his shoulders.

Cora knew them both well enough to understand what they each meant when they said those words. Kyle was just excited. He found a way to get excited about almost everything, from lost pets to sorting glass and plastic bottles.

Sybella was in awe. *Fifth. Grade.* They had made it so far, all the way to the top of the school.

The little kids buzzed past them, and Cora wondered if she had ever looked so ridiculously, supremely happy. She had felt that way once, probably, but not recently. Definitely not since her mother had moved out over the summer and gone all the way to Belgium, where the time difference made it harder for Cora to talk to her mom in real time. They had video chats as often as they could, but it wasn't the same. Cora had started leaving public service announcements on her mom's voicemail just as a way of saying, "I'm still here."

"Touch the Toad for luck," Sybella said, and they reached out to touch the iron skin of the Marshall Toad, the sculpture of their mascot that sat on a pedestal by the main door.

This year, the three Aquafabians were spread out in three different fifth-grade classrooms. When they got to the fifth-grade wing, they put their hands out, one on top of the other.

"*Aquafaba,*" said Cora.

"*Patria,*" said Sybella.

"*Est,*" said Kyle.

They split up and jostled through the crowd to their classrooms. Cora paused in the doorway to Room 245 and turned to see if she could catch Sybella's eye and give a final salute. But Sybella was being swept along toward her classroom with no space to turn and look back at Cora. She disappeared into Room 247, followed by a sea of kids.

They'd been in different classes before, but Cora had really wanted to be in the same class for their last year at Marshall. A grumpy cloud settled over her as she found her seat, which had a label that said *CORA* and a picture of a sea lion. She thought she might be too old to have a sea lion on her desk, but the sea lion was cute. Sybella had set Cora's and Kyle's text notifications as a sea lion bark when she'd gotten her phone in fourth grade. Thinking of that pushed a little of Cora's grumpiness away.

She was close to the front of the room, but she didn't mind it the way some kids did. It meant she was closer to the door. Closer to Kyle and Sybella. Once everyone was sitting down, Ms. Nuñez turned out the lights. It was bright outside, so the classroom only went a little dim, but everyone got quiet and looked toward the front of the room.

"Fifth. Grade," said Ms. Nuñez, and Cora wished Sybella was there to hear that. "You've made it, you guys. You should be proud. Fifth grade is a big year. You're going to look back at how far you've come, and you're going to look ahead at what's coming up. We'll visit Le Guin Middle School in the spring to help you think about the future, and you'll get a second-grade reading buddy in a few weeks, so you can share your knowledge but also to help you remember where you came from."

Cora traced her sea lion with her finger while she half-listened. She didn't have to think about where she came from or where she was going, because she knew where she belonged. Right next to Kyle and Sybella.

In fourth grade, Kyle had started to spend some recesses volunteering in the library or in the garden, but that was okay. Cora knew that she still had Kyle at home and Sybella at school, and that their world was safe. It would always be there for them, and they would never ask anyone else to join, because even though Aquafaba was anywhere and everywhere and stretched as far as you could see, it still only had room for three people.

"Let's talk about our theme words for the year," Ms. Nuñez went on. She pointed to a paper banner that hung on one side of the classroom.

Community. Self-direction. Sustainability.

They talked about what each of the words meant and why they were good ones to focus on that year. When they got to sustainability, Cora started looking impatiently at the clock.

She knew what sustainability meant because her parents talked about it all the time. They talked about it separately, now that they were getting divorced. In July, Cora's mother had moved out of their apartment in California to work at a university in Belgium for a year while she "thought about the future." But even with all that distance between them, her parents still found a way to talk about exactly the same things.

Kids used to ask Cora if her parents were trash collectors—that is, the people who picked up curbside trash in a giant garbage truck. They weren't, although sometimes Cora wished they were. At least trash collectors had somewhere to put all the trash they collected. They didn't bring it home.

Her garbologist parents didn't just study how

garbage was produced, or which recycling bin it should go into, but what actually happened to it after the trucks picked it up from the transfer station. Did recyclables really get recycled? How long did it take? Where did they go? What were the most common things in landfills? They tracked and mapped it all, using TrashTrack, an app her mom had designed.

Her mom, who had once been Dr. Clare Davis but was now going back to being Dr. Clare Wilson, was studying how cities in Europe handled their waste, and she showed them how to use her app to track it. Her dad, Dr. Duncan Davis, had been on a mission, since long before Cora and Kyle were born, to show the world what happened to the things it tried to get rid of. And he almost always brought his work home with him. He even went through the trash in their apartment building regularly to make sure as little as possible was going directly to the landfill. Cora often found a bag of trash in the bathtub, waiting for him and his blue rubber gloves.

Cora did not need lessons on sustainability.

At first recess, she ran to the playground to wait for Kyle and Sybella. She sat on a low bench underneath the main structure, and soon Kyle came to sit next to her.

"Mr. Chee says we're going to do community projects this year, and I asked if my community project could be washing dogs at the Humane Society, and he said yes!"

Nothing made Kyle more excited than dogs. "Do you think Dad will take me on Saturdays? I think there's a bus that goes near there. Or we could ride bikes."

Dr. Davis didn't have a car, but he had told the twins that he *might* consider getting one if he could make it run on biogas made from their own food scraps. "If you want a car, you'll need to start eating more vegetables," he'd said.

Sybella appeared then. "Hey, Kyle," she said, pretending not to see Cora and sitting on her lap. Cora laughed.

"You could get hurt doing that," said someone in a voice that was whiny and gravelly at the same time. Cora couldn't see past Sybella to tell who it was. "Do you have playground monitors at this school? My old school had playground monitors, and they would be on you in a hot second."

Sybella was giggling so hard she slid off Cora's lap onto the ground. A girl Cora didn't recognize was standing under the structure in a dress that looked like an enormous plaid shirt, cinched at the waist with a sequined belt. She had frizzy blond hair and pale, blotchy skin. "At my old school," the girl continued, "we had avocado toast for school breakfast."

"That sounds . . . great," said Kyle. Kyle couldn't help trying to be friendly.

Cora could help it. She had years of practice not being very friendly. Not because she wanted to be *un*friendly, just because it had never been easy to be friends with anyone except Sybella. And Kyle, who made everything easy.

Sybella caught Cora's eye and gave a tiny nod. She said, "Let's go to the climbing wall!" She stood up and took off across the playground. Cora and Kyle followed, and so did the girl in the plaid dress.

"At my old school, we had mindfulness meditation for gym," she said, breathing hard. When the Aquafabians tried to escape to the swings, she ran after them, saying, "At my old school, we didn't have swings because a kid flew off and broke his front teeth."

Eventually, when the three Aquafabians realized that the playground wasn't big enough to lose someone completely, they gave up and stopped running. The girl caught her breath and kept talking.

Mr. Sheehy, Sybella's teacher, wandered over and said, "I'm glad to see you're making friends, Marnie. Cora and Kyle, Marnie Stoll is new here this year, and I know you'll help her feel right at home at Marshall. Sybella, thank you for showing our new student the ropes."

"At my old school we had ropes, but they were only for mooring the school yacht," said Marnie, and then the bell rang.

Cora tried to dawdle on the way to line up, hoping that Marnie would be the kind of kid who wanted to be first in line. And she was. She started running toward the line, and Cora said to Sybella, "School yacht?"

"I bet they didn't have a yacht. She's in my class, and she was talking like that all morning."

"She's not going to follow us around every recess, is she?"

Sybella shrugged, and then Marnie came running back to them. "At my old school, it was an honor to be first in line," she said. "But I guess not every school is like my old school. Hey, what's for lunch today? At my old school we had halibut on Mondays. Do you have halibut on Mondays here? I'll sit with you at lunch, okay?"

Who cared what was for lunch when the bigger problem was that this new girl, Marnie, not only wouldn't leave them alone at recess but also wanted to sit with them at lunch? What if she followed them at every recess and crowded in on them at every lunch? It was a small thing, but it felt like a crack in the walls of their kingdom, or a cloud of dust on the horizon, kicked up by an invading army.

Ever since second grade, when the world of Aquafaba had expanded just enough to let Sybella in and then closed again to keep everyone else out, they had mostly played by themselves. They weren't being rude, and they weren't being left out of things. Playing together was just what they did, and everyone seemed to understand it—except Marnie.

Cora wished, then, that they had taken the time to invent a complete language instead of code words, because she needed to talk to Sybella. She tried to think of a code word that would say everything she needed to say, but then Sybella said it for her: "Broccoli."

Cora lit up, and she nodded. "Broccoli!"

"That's weird," said Marnie. "Just broccoli? Steamed? Stir fried? Broccoli is gross, anyway. It's a good thing I brought a lunch because . . ."

Cora didn't listen to Marnie's description of her lunch. She went to her line, feeling lucky to have a friend who understood her so well and thinking for the hundred zillionth time that Sybella was the best friend a person could ever have.

Sybella had come up with the code word *broccoli* when they were naming places back in second grade. They needed a word for the library, because the library was a great secret meeting place. You could go there when you were done with your seatwork to get a new book, and your best friend might ask to go there at exactly the same time, because you'd said "Broccoli" to each other before you sat down in class.

You could also eat lunch in the library if you promised

to put away one stack of books afterward. And that was Sybella's plan. When lunchtime came later in the day, they would meet there to eat, shelve books, and avoid Marnie Stoll.

When recess was over, Cora and Kyle went to their classrooms, and Marnie followed Sybella into their classroom, chatting about yachts. As soon as Cora took her seat again, Ms. Nuñez kept right on going with the sustainability theme.

"Sustainability is about the planet, but it's also about you," she said. "It's about how you fit into all these big systems—water, climate, food, everything—and how we can all make sure that the next generations have what they need. Can anyone give me an example of sustainability? Big or small?"

Kids raised their hands, waving them at Ms. Nuñez. Cora stared at the door and then at her cubby. She thought about the banana sandwich she'd brought for her lunch. Banana sandwiches were her mom's favorite. Did they have banana sandwiches in Belgium?

"Cora? Can you give an example?"

She could have given a hundred examples. Every Saturday she dragged large reusable containers to the bulk foods section of her dad's favorite grocery store, the Berkeley Bowl, on the bus. She and Kyle had to share a phone—they called it the Twin Phone—because phones made e-waste, and Dr. Davis hated e-waste. He had let their mother buy them a single phone so they could stay in touch while she was gone, but only after showing them a documentary about how American e-waste was polluting the environment and ruining people's health in countries like Ghana in West Africa, where it was sent to be recycled. She could have starred in a whole series of web videos about how to save the earth.

But Cora had learned long ago that even in Berkeley, where you could buy eight different kinds of organic apples and there'd been a guy on the news who composted food in his pockets, there was a limit to how much people wanted to hear about garbage. In second grade, she'd stood by the garbage can in the cafeteria for a whole lunch period, helpfully telling people what was supposed to go in each bin and making them have do-overs when they got it wrong. None of the kids had appreciated her expertise, and even her teacher, Ms. Reynolds, finally suggested that maybe she should make a poster instead.

So when Ms. Nuñez asked her for an example, all she said was, "Like, making waffles from scratch instead of buying them frozen?" Cora was good at making waffles—she *loved* waffles—but by trying too hard not to sound like a know-it-all, she sounded like she didn't know anything.

Ms. Nuñez made the face grown-ups make when they think you're trying your best but your best isn't very good and said, "Sure. That's a good one. Anyone else?"

At least the broccoli plan worked perfectly. Cora had whispered it to Kyle before he went to his class, so all three Aquafabians met there at lunchtime. They sat on the steps of the Reading Corner and spread their food out, picnic style.

"Should we eat lunch here every day?" asked Cora. "Just to be safe?" She liked the library, but she wasn't sure about spending the rest of the year shelving books instead of playing outside.

"Maybe for a couple of days," said Sybella. "She probably just needs to find her place, and then she'll stop bugging us. But we don't always need to change what *we* do for *her*."

Sybella took a bite of her tandoori chicken wrap, and Cora peeled the waxed paper from her banana sandwich. It felt good to hear Sybella say that, as if somehow she knew they were going to be fine.

That good feeling stayed with Cora through the rest of the school day. At 2:25, the last bell rang. Cora, Kyle, and Sybella met in the hall and made their way past the streams of kids to the cafeteria for the After-School Fair.

Every year on the first day of school, kids who stayed for after-school care could see displays about all the clubs and activities the school offered and choose which ones to sign up for. The Aquafabians usually skipped the organized activities and spent their afternoons on the playground, but this year Dr. Davis had already made sure his children were signed up for the one after-school activity that mattered: the one he had designed and that his graduate students were running. Of course, it was all about garbage.

"At my old school, we had an after-school club for learning how to fly hot-air balloons," said Marnie, catching up to them. Obviously she hadn't found her place yet. "And horse racing."

"You know what's the most fun thing here? At *this* school?" said Sybella. "Playing outside. Maybe you should just play on the playground instead?"

"My mom says I need to 'fit in,'" said Marnie, making air quotes with her fingers. "She says I have to join a club, even if it's more boring than the clubs at my old school."

"I scream, you scream, we all scream for Trash Team!" said Kyle, shimmying toward the cafeteria table with the giant recycling logo poster.

Cora was not screaming for Trash Team. But at least Dani would be there.

Dani de la Cruz was one of Dr. Davis's research assistants. Cora and Kyle had met her several times at their dad's Trash Lab last year. Dani wasn't like anyone else Cora knew. She was a little grumpy sometimes, a little cynical, but good and kind in ways that were less obvious. And she made working with trash almost . . . fun.

Dani, wearing skinny jeans and a black tank top, was sitting on one of the cafeteria tables, reading something on her phone. When Cora, Sybella, and Kyle walked up to the table, with Marnie close behind, she looked up and smiled. She had never met Sybella, and Cora was excited to introduce them.

"Hey, guys," said Dani.

"Hey," said Cora. "This is Sybella! Remember, I told you about her?"

"For two hours," said Dani, grinning. "I remember." To Sybella, she said, "Cora talks about you a lot."

"And I'm Marnie Stoll." Marnie held her hand out to Dani. "I'm also Cora's very good friend. She hasn't told you anything about me yet because we just met, but she probably will. Or I could tell you myself. At my old school—"

"Any friend of Cora's is a friend of mine," said Dani, shaking Marnie's hand, but Cora thought she saw a question in Dani's expression. Cora had to stop herself from saying, "She's not my friend! I barely even know her!"

"I like your tattoos," said Sybella, a little shyly.

Ink spread on Dani's arms like patterns in a coloring book in tiny, intricate circles and waves and flowers. If Cora squinted and tilted her head, she thought she could see words hidden in the lines: *Today; Ayer,* which she knew was Spanish for "yesterday"; *Alma,* or maybe *Anna*. A pattern Cora hadn't seen before crept past Dani's elbow. She was always adding pieces to it.

Dani made a face. "Never get a tattoo on the inside of your elbow," she said. "It hurts."

"Someone at my old school died from an infected tattoo," said Marnie.

"Wow," said Dani, sounding a little like Ms. Nuñez when Cora talked about waffles. To Cora and Kyle, she said, "Your dad's probably making you join the trash project, right?"

Cora nodded glumly, and Kyle nodded enthusiastically. "Is Juniper here too?" he asked. "He was teaching me how to juggle."

Juniper was another research assistant and possibly Kyle's favorite person who wasn't family or Sybella. He liked dogs too, and besides juggling, he could walk on his hands and ride a unicycle. Kyle wanted to do all those things. Kyle would join any club if Juniper was there.

Dani slid off the table and started unpacking a box. Cora knew that box. It had one of every kind of recyclable thing, plus some things that were not recyclable. Dr. Davis and his students used it for all their school and community programs. Dani set a soda can on the table next to an old leather boot. "Yeah, he's here, but he's not juggling today."

"I beg to differ," said Juniper, appearing in the doorway in a tie-dye T-shirt that read *Save the Snails*. "I am *always* juggling." As if to prove it, he took three hacky sacks from the pockets of his shorts and tossed them into the air, sending them up higher and faster, and even catching them behind his back. "Ready?"

Kyle nodded. One by one, Juniper sent the hacky sacks to Kyle, and one by one, Kyle dropped them on the floor.

"We'll keep working on it," said Juniper. "But for now . . ." He held out his hands to Dani as if he was presenting her to everyone. Dani snorted.

"I'm Dani, and this is Juniper. We work in the Trash Lab at the university, which is as cool-slash-gross as it sounds. Your school is participating in a project where we track trash at local schools to see how much stuff you guys are recycling and how much you're throwing away. If you decide to join the Trash Team, we'll meet here on Fridays. We'll count and measure all the different types of trash your school produces, and we'll learn what happens to your trash after you throw it away. We have some other fun activities about sustainability planned too."

Cora knew all about tracking trash. Her own trash had been tracked last spring by one of Dr. Davis's research teams. It was really something to know that the things you tried to throw away would never actually leave you. Or they wouldn't ever leave your mind, at least, because months after you'd recycled something, some grad student was going to tell you exactly where it was and how long it had been there.

"You can learn a lot that way!" said Juniper. "Cora here recycled an Orange Juice Jam bottle seventeen weeks ago, and it's still sitting in a truck outside a facility in Colorado!"

"Isn't that thing ever going to get recycled?" said Cora.

"The recycling program at my old school—" began Marnie.

"It's wild, huh?" said Juniper. "You throw something in a recycling bin and you think it's just going to get turned into a park bench—*poof*! But the laws of garbage don't always work like that. Sometimes the trackers show us that stuff doesn't move for weeks or at all. The system's not as efficient as it should be."

Dani walked them through each type of recycling or trash and explained how the project worked. "Each week, we'll go through each bin and count everything and record it all in a database. We'll choose a few things to put tracking tags on and then we'll follow them on the tracking app to see where they go."

She held out her phone, which was open to the tracking app. Cora had seen it a million times before. It showed the path each item took, from wherever it had started to its final destination. When she'd looked at the map of all the things Dr. Davis's team had tracked, it was like looking at a map of airplane routes or highways, red lines going everywhere. Trash had an amazing secret life. Cora wondered if she would ever travel as far as her trash did.

Dani handed a tracking tag to Sybella, who looked at it carefully and passed it to someone else. It was small, about the size of a domino. "This is basically the guts of a cell phone," said Dani. "When we attach it to a piece of trash, like this, we can follow where it goes on an app called TrashTrack that reads cell phone signals." She held up the old boot and tucked another tracker into the space behind the label that was sewn into the tongue. She squeezed in some glue to keep it in place. "If I had two boots, I wouldn't be throwing them away, by the way. But I just found this one in a trash can down the street, so I brought it along because it's a great example of an unusual piece of trash. This tag is designed to turn on every couple of hours when it's moving and send out a signal, and it keeps doing that until the battery dies or it goes out of cell phone range. This will be one of the items we'll track, and starting next week we'll get some more pieces from the trash cans here and put trackers on them."

"So if it's not moving, it just sits there?" asked Derrick, a kid in Sybella's class.

"Yeah, and it sleeps to save battery."

"This sounds boring," said Marnie. Cora waited for her to go to another table, but she stayed put.

"Do you get the trackers back when the trash gets to where it's supposed to go?" asked Derrick.

"No, they stay with the item we're tracking. They're safe enough to go in the landfill, so if that's where the item goes, it's okay."

"So it's like GPS?" asked someone else.

"Sort of, but it doesn't use satellites. It uses cell towers, so we can get better signals inside buildings," Dani explained.

Kids passed the tag around. One of the third graders put it on her head, saying robotically, "I. Am. Garbage." Another kid swiped it off the girl's head and the crowd started chanting, "Here, here!" The tag went high into the air, and before anyone could catch it, Juniper grabbed it and held it out of everyone's reach.

Dani waited for the group to quiet down. "If you like throwing electronics around the cafeteria, you're going to love this next part. In April, we're having a couple of special events to celebrate Earth Day. These are open to everyone, even if you're not part of Trash Team. First up is the Trashlympics on the Saturday before Earth Day."

"It's going to be awesome!" said Juniper. "There'll be Capture the Trash, the triashlon, and trash-and-field events! It's a festival of trashletics for all you young trashletes!"

Some of the kids laughed. "Like, we're going to play basketball with trash and stuff?" said Waleed, who was in Cora's class.

"Trashketball!" said someone else.

"We should totally add trashketball," said Juniper, pretending to shoot a basket. Kids cheered.

Dani did a teacher clap, five times quickly, to get everyone to be quiet again. "There's also a Trash-In, which is a giant trash-sorting event, kind of like what we're doing here with your school trash. You know how you have all those containers at home for different kinds of trash—stuff you can recycle, stuff you can compost, and stuff you just throw away? What we want you to do is bring us those containers. Full of trash. Whatever is in them, we want to see it. Except the really gross stuff."

"First you STASH your TRASH, then we dump it—CRASH!" sang Juniper.

"And we sort it by category and prepare a statistical analysis of the waste removal stream," said Dani.

"That doesn't rhyme," said Marnie.

"That's right," said Dani. "Annnnyway, bring us all your trash—"

Juniper raised his arm like the Statue of Liberty. "Bring us your tired, your poor, your huddled trashes, yearning to be sorted. The wretched refuse of your teeming bins—"

"But not until April," continued Dani. "Then you and your team—"

"Trash Team! Team Trash!" Juniper waved imaginary pom-poms. Next to Cora, Kyle waved imaginary pom-poms too, almost as if he wasn't thinking about it. As if he was just really enjoying the presentation, while some of the other kids giggled or moved away.

"—can help us sort it all and figure out how successful the city's home-based zero waste program is," Dani finished saying as she started passing out flyers. "This has all the information about the project, including the Upcycle Your Trash art contest, which is the Saturday after the Trashlympics."

Cora didn't take a flyer, because she already knew everything there was to know about the events and also because it would just give her one more thing to recycle later.

"Uh, what are trash points?" asked a second grader in a unicorn hoodie, pointing to the flyer.

"Trash points are like gold!" said Juniper. "You earn them all year long for coming to Trash Team meetings, sorting trash, and bringing your trash to the Trash-In. You get one hundred trash points if you stay and sort trash, and the Trashlympics has a point system for each event. And you can earn more trash points by participating in the art contest."

"That's . . . a lot of trash," said the second grader. She sounded a little overwhelmed.

"You can trade your trash points for exciting trash-related prizes!" added Juniper.

"What's a trash-related prize?" asked Marnie. She snatched a flyer from the kid next to her, looking interested for the first time. "I didn't know there would be prizes."

"It's all in the flyer," said Dani. "And the person with the most trash points wins the grand prize: a research trip on the bay to collect fish data."

"What's that?" asked Sybella.

"Data about fish, I guess?" said Dani.

"How is that a prize?" asked Marnie.

Privately, Cora agreed. She'd had her share of

educational presents, but this seemed like a new low.

"How is it not a prize?" Juniper threw his arms out, as if he couldn't understand how anyone wouldn't be over the moon to collect fish data, whatever it was. "It's fish! Data! A free trip on the beautiful San Francisco Bay! Come on!"

Cora could tell most of the kids were skeptical of the value of this grand prize. There were sighs, and muttered "Whatevers," and not a lot of excitement.

Dani shrugged as if to say, "That's it," while Juniper did a high kick and a cartwheel, nearly crashing into one of the large cafeteria garbage cans. He ended by lifting the can and holding it high in the air, as if that's what he'd meant to do all along.

Some of the kids drifted off to other parts of the cafeteria, where teachers were waiting with trifold boards about robotics or gaming or art. Some asked Juniper to do another cartwheel, or tried their own, which got them sent out onto the playground.

Sybella looked at a few of the other displays.

"I didn't know Ms. Jackson ran a chess club on Fridays," she said. Ms. Jackson, the school librarian, was wearing a tall black hat with a horse's head on top. "Oh, I get it. She's the knight." Sybella laughed. "Chess is kind of fun. I wonder what the club's like."

"I was thinking of doing chess," said Marnie.

Cora's shoulders locked. It was one thing if Sybella wanted to do chess. Cora would pout, because she couldn't help it, but you couldn't keep a friend away from something that made her happy. But if she was going to have to spend her Friday afternoons wearing blue rubber gloves and watching kids wear trash trackers on their heads, she wanted Sybella to be there too. Not doing chess. With *Marnie.*

Cora had only known Marnie for three hours, and already it felt like three long and awful years.

"I'm not doing chess," said Sybella. Cora's shoulders relaxed. "I was just looking around. I'm doing Trash Team." She put one arm around Cora and one around Kyle. "We're all doing Trash Team."

"I mean, that's what I'm doing," said Marnie. "I'm doing Trash Team too."

Ugh.

For a moment, Cora and Sybella just looked at each other. Then, a tall woman in a long, purple coat appeared behind Marnie. "Time to go, Angel Puff," she said, guiding Marnie away. "How was your first day?"

"At my old school . . . ," said Marnie, but by then she was too far away for Cora to hear anything else she said.

Cora turned to Sybella, and Sybella let out a long

wheeeew. "Maybe we should eat lunch in broccoli for, like, a month."

"Yeah," Cora agreed. A little nervously, she pointed at Ms. Jackson's hat. "Do you really want to do chess?" she asked.

"Kind of," said Sybella. "But I know you have to do this, and I'd rather be with you."

"Maybe you can do both," said Kyle. "Chess meets Wednesdays *and* Fridays. Maybe you can do chess on Wednesdays and Trash Team on Fridays?"

"You sure can," said Ms. Jackson, her knight's hat bobbing. "And if you need extra practice, we can figure something out for you."

"Really?" asked Sybella, her smile showing all her teeth. "Thank you!"

"That's what I call a winning strategy!" said Ms. Jackson. Sybella laughed, because Sybella always laughed at teacher jokes. "In fact, why don't I take you over to the library right now, and I'll find *Queen of Katwe* for you. It's a great chess movie—it'll get you in a chess mood before our first meeting next week."

Sybella grinned again.

"Do you want to join too?" Ms. Jackson asked Cora and Kyle. "I love seeing you all being such good friends. You've been a tight little crew for years!"

Now Cora grinned, because it was true. "I don't

know if I'm going to do chess, but we're never going to stop being friends," she said to Ms. Jackson.

"That's good," said Ms. Jackson. "You keep it that way."

Cora

After

DR. CLARE WILSON'S VOICEMAIL

Twin Phone

"This is another public service announcement. The City of Berkeley is announcing a new waste management program. Beginning immediately, you may place all your feelings in a curbside bin for pickup. The bin will be barf green, because that is the color of all your feelings mixed together. We will take them away, out of sight, so far away you won't ever have to worry about them again. Actually, you won't be able to worry about anything, because after we take the bin you won't have any feelings left. Not even worry. Thank you for listening to this important announcement."

Speaker Call Back Delete

"Is everyone ready?" Dr. Davis asked. "Cora? Kyle? Sybella?"

Cora had begged. She had complained. She had tried being grouchy, grumpy, unpleasant, disagreeable, willful, snarky, rude, and obnoxious. She had tried hiding Dr. Davis's wallet, pretending to come down with a cold, and lying flat on her face, refusing to answer to anyone.

None of it worked. Sybella's mother was traveling to a conference this weekend, like she did every year in spring, and her dad was at a college reunion, so even though she and Cora hadn't said a word to each other in two weeks, Sybella was coming to Auntie Lake's for the weekend.

Auntie Lake wasn't really Cora's aunt. She was an

old friend of Dr. Davis's family, older than he was but not quite old enough to be Cora's grandmother. She acted as an honorary aunt, which was useful because Dr. Davis and Dr. Wilson had no siblings, and Cora loved spending the weekend in Auntie Lake's cozy, comfortable house across the bay in Sausalito. They always streamed episodes of TV shows from the seventies and eighties, when everyone had bad hair and wore interestingly terrible clothing, and Auntie Lake let them have hot chocolate and waffles for dinner. It was due to Auntie Lake that Cora was so good at making waffles.

Cora should have been overjoyed. She *had been* overjoyed about the idea when the Aquafabians were still planning to have their centennial celebration.

They'd thought of it a couple of weeks ago in March, while they were playing Hopscotch on the playground at lunch recess. They'd stopped eating lunch in broccoli—Marnie had found them there after a week. Sybella had admitted that she felt a little sorry for Marnie, who was not having an easy time fitting in. So now sometimes Marnie attached herself to them, and sometimes she attached herself to some other group.

She wasn't with the Aquafabians the day they talked about their centennial. It was funny, really, that although they played and used code words less than they used to, they felt more attached to their world now that Marnie loomed around its edges. So they planned a party for themselves, because they could.

"Doesn't *centennial* mean hundredth birthday?" Kyle had asked. "Aquafaba's not a hundred years old."

"No, but you don't have a really big celebration for a fourth birthday," Cora had said. "And we're really advanced in Aquafaba."

Cora couldn't think of a better place to hold their celebration than Auntie Lake's house, and Auntie Lake was happy to have them. It was decided. They would invite Sybella over for a weekend, and they would bring all their centennial party supplies with them.

Cora and Kyle turned down the idea of buying hundredth birthday paper plates and cups and napkins because they said it was wasteful. For the same reason, they all said no to streamers, balloons, glitter, anything made of Mylar, noisemakers, and ten-for-a-dollar plastic party favors that came in plastic bags.

They all said yes to a cake, because it was cake, and yes to homemade decorations using aluminum cans, newspaper, brown paper bags, and some of the thick, lumpy paper they had made at Juniper's Eco-Craft Camp during winter break. They would also make friendship bracelets ahead of time and wear them while they made all the other decorations.

Aquafaba had no official colors, so they made

friendship bracelets in every color of embroidery thread in the Stellar Suzy Friendship Bracelet Factory kit Sybella had been given for Christmas. They made the Fishtail and the Stripe and the Twist, and Kyle tried the Paw Print, but the paws came out looking like mud puddles.

The funny thing about friendship bracelets was that you could tie them on easily, but it was harder to get them off. The knots got too tight, and the threads got mashed together if you ever wore them in the shower. With bracelets stacked on each arm, the Aquafabians had a lot of tight knots and mashed threads, but they didn't mind. *Aquafaba patria est.* They were wearing the flags of their country.

The centennial celebration wasn't going to happen until early in April. They'd thought about waiting a couple of weeks and having it on their triple birthday instead, but then they realized they could have another party for that later on. They finished all their homemade decorations, and they agreed that everything looked very nice. Not shiny, maybe. Not glittery. But very nice.

But that was two weeks ago. Now that they weren't friends anymore, there was nothing left to celebrate, but they had to spend the weekend together anyway. Cora had thrown all the decorations they'd made in the trash and then, when she'd calmed down, she took them out and put them in the recycling. But she'd taken a picture of it anyway and started a text to Sybella, saying, I guess there's no party now. She'd erased it before she could send it.

Cora wanted to talk to someone about what had happened, but she didn't know how to talk about it or who to talk to. When she woke up feeling sad at seven o'clock in the morning, it was four in the afternoon in Belgium, and her mom was still at work, and when she went to bed feeling sad at nine o'clock at night, her mom was still asleep. She wanted to talk to Kyle, but Kyle wouldn't understand that you could be friends one day and not friends the next, or that you could feel like a good person one day and the next day you didn't know how to feel. Take three friends and subtract one, and somehow you were left with nothing.

"She's still your friend. You could talk to her," Kyle had said.

"You're wrong," said Cora. "She doesn't want to be my friend anymore. She probably doesn't want to be your friend anymore, either." She felt mean, saying that, but sometimes she wished Kyle wasn't always so determined to look for every bright side.

Kyle saw the good in everything, and he always wanted to believe the best. He believed the lie that grown-ups tell children about the strength of friendship.

The truth was, friendship wasn't strong. It was brittle, breakable, like a tiny shell. It was slimy and slipped through your fingers like seaweed. It didn't last, and if Kyle thought it did, then maybe he was still living in an imaginary kingdom. But during all their troubles, somehow, the gates of Aquafaba had been closed and locked, and they were all on the outside.

Now they were all on the ferry to Sausalito together, and Auntie Lake was going to pick them up at the dock. Cora wished for once that it wasn't so far away, or that they had at least been able to drive instead of taking the ferry, which would have been fun before, but was now slow and miserable. Dr. Davis was along for the ride, but he would get on the next ferry back to San Francisco and take the train home.

"Do you think we can still do the Trashlympics together?" asked Kyle. "It's only a couple of weeks away. I don't know if we can find new teams in time."

Kyle was a peacemaker. He didn't fight, and he even helped other kids solve their playground fights. He didn't seem to think what had happened between Cora and Sybella was that bad—and that was just one more thing for Cora to feel angry about. "No," said Cora. "We're not a team. Not anymore." She felt bad, but Kyle would find a new team. He was good at things like that.

Sybella sat next to Dr. Davis, who was talking about plastic in the oceans and how some scientists were trying to clean up the stuff on the surface, but that nobody knew how to clean up all the stuff beneath the surface. Underneath, everything broke down into tiny pieces that were hard to see and hard to remove. When fish and other ocean animals swallowed ocean water, they swallowed plastic too. It sat there in their stomachs until they died.

"The real danger of ocean plastic," said Dr. Davis, "isn't what you can see, it's what you can't see."

That sounded about right to Cora: Her life had been upended by problems she'd never seen coming.

She grabbed Kyle's hand and found them seats on the other side of the ferry. A few rays of sunlight tried to break through the clouds, but mostly everything was dull and gray, which perfectly matched how Cora felt.

She still thought about Aquafaba, even though she tried her hardest not to. The thing about it that she had loved so much was how it could completely surround you just because you started thinking about it. The air would suddenly shimmer and bend, and you could travel far, far away without moving an inch.

But not anymore.

"I hate everything," said Cora. "I hate everything so much."

"I know you do," said Kyle. Cora had said that a lot recently.

"Everything except you," she said quickly, even though she was sure Kyle knew that he was always the exception.

"I know that too."

Auntie Lake met them at the ferry dock, and they said goodbye to Dr. Davis. In the car on the way to Auntie Lake's house, Cora tried to imagine what it would feel like to be flotsam, to be a piece of plastic floating on the surface of the ocean. Or to have the cold ocean close over her and leave her floating dangerously underneath. To be there, but not to be seen.

"I've been looking forward to this celebration," Auntie Lake said as she drove. "Do you have all your party things in those little backpacks?" Cora realized that, after talking to her about it for weeks, she had forgotten to tell her that the celebration was off.

Sybella was in the front seat, and Cora elbowed Kyle, trying to say with her eyes everything she couldn't say out loud.

Kyle caught on. "Oh, um, that already happened. So we didn't need to bring anything."

Sybella twisted in her seat and made a face Cora couldn't figure out. Surprised? Sad? Confused?

Auntie Lake said, "Oh." It was obvious she didn't

believe Kyle, but she didn't ask any more questions. Instead she pointed out things along the way to Sybella and told stories about growing up in the days before cell phones.

"We had to communicate through tin cans tied to a string," said Auntie Lake.

"Really?" said Sybella, sounding as if she didn't believe a word of it.

"Well, just for fun. But you had to be pretty close to each other to use them. In the same house, at least. You couldn't have a string going all the way from your house to your friend's house across town."

Cora imagined a city crisscrossed by strings, lines going everywhere, house to house to house. Kyle must have thought of the same thing, because he said, "A million tin can phones stretched across a city would look like the map on TrashTrack."

"It would," agreed Auntie Lake. "Imagine, a million ways to connect to people, and yet sometimes it's still impossible."

No one said anything after that.

Auntie Lake turned into her driveway. Usually the sight of her house and the persimmon tree in her yard made Cora sigh with happiness. She and Kyle had spent a lot of time there last summer, when Dr. Davis and Dr. Davis (soon to be Dr. Wilson) were working out the details of their divorce. Auntie Lake had swooped down to carry the children to a place of peacefulness and safety, like a miraculous fairy-tale bird. The air had shimmered there once, but today it, too, was dull and gray. Cora looked, but she couldn't see anything beyond the ordinary. How had a place that had been an escape from her problems suddenly become the same as everywhere else?

When they went to put their backpacks away in the upstairs guest rooms, Cora realized that she and Sybella were sharing a room. They had the room with two twin beds, and Kyle had the room with only one bed. Usually, Cora fought Kyle for the room with two beds, so she could jump back and forth, pretending the beds were rocks and the space between them was an enchanted river. If she slipped into the water, she would be under a spell. But the room, like everything else, looked ordinary now.

She said, "Kyle, do you want to share? We could give Sybella a room to herself because she's the guest."

She hoped Auntie Lake would appreciate how generous she was being, but Auntie Lake said no. She still didn't ask questions, but she firmly directed Cora and Sybella to their room.

"You can have the bed by the window," said Cora. Not because she was being generous, but because she would be closer to the door, and that would make it easier to get away.

"Thanks." Sybella's voice came out in a whisper.

Cora dumped her backpack on the other bed and ran downstairs, leaving Sybella alone to unpack.

In the living room, Auntie Lake had set out a thousand-piece puzzle, a box of oil pastels and a large pad of paper, and—Cora's favorite—building blocks made of real stone. There were regular, flat pieces as well as cylinders and arches and turrets, some with lines etched in them to make them look like groups of bricks. Kyle fell to work on the puzzle, and Cora flopped down on the floor with the blocks. If anyone at school had seen her playing with blocks, she would have pointed to the case, which said they were architectural blocks from Germany, and they were helping her build a foundation of three-dimensional mathematics, but privately, she just liked the feel of them. Real stone, as if she were a giant, building tiny underwater castles for mermaids.

Sybella stood shyly in the living room doorway, and Auntie Lake gestured to her to come in. "Sit with me," she said. "Maybe you can help me with something."

She reached for a small wooden box from one of her built-in shelves. Flowers and vines were carved delicately into its surface. "This silly little lock. I can't open it. Do you want to give it a try? There's a small key, and it used to turn perfectly and open right up, but I've lost the knack. Old fingers, I guess."

"Okay," said Sybella. She turned the box around to examine it. "Where's the key? Where's the lock?"

Auntie Lake laughed. "There are panels in the front and back. Slide them open and look."

The box was like a puzzle, but Sybella solved it easily. She found the tiny key and the lock. She put the key in and tried turning it one way, then the other, but it wouldn't catch.

"What's in the box?" asked Kyle, looking up from his puzzle.

Auntie Lake gave a little shrug. "Oh, I can hardly remember."

"Murex!" said Kyle. Sybella turned to stare at him. "Murex, murex, murex."

Obviously Kyle hadn't given up on Aquafaba, but then Kyle never gave up on anything. *Murex* was one of their secret words. It was a purple dye made from the mucous secretions of predatory sea snails. It was something only royalty could use, from a long time ago when dye was expensive and rare. They had decided, therefore, that it was Aquafabian for "good fortune" and possibly "riches." It was a good word for opening locked things that might be full of riches, because predatory sea snails had tried to lock themselves up in their fancy shells, but it hadn't worked.

Now that they weren't really talking to each other, their code words sat unused.

Where do words go when you're done with them? Cora wondered. *Who keeps track of them after that?*

Sybella tilted her head, as if the air around her was bending and shimmering and she was trying to see into another world. "Murex!" she said. She whispered it again, three times, and turned the key.

The lock clicked. Magic. True, Auntie Lake's house was a magical place, and Auntie Lake herself was a little magical, and even the damp, misty ocean air swirled like it was coming straight out of a book on King Arthur, but Cora wondered if their Aquafabian words had something to do with it too. Auntie Lake smiled at Sybella.

"Go ahead, open it."

Sybella lifted the carved lid. Her forehead wrinkled, and Auntie Lake leaned over to look inside the box. She picked up something very small and fragile and laid it on her palm. A friendship bracelet.

There were more of them in the box. The bracelets looked old, as if they'd been worn often, but long ago. Now their colors were faded, and the embroidery thread was fuzzy and fraying. Some of the bracelets had been untied to remove them, and some had been cut straight through the middle.

Auntie Lake picked up an orange-and-yellow one. "We used to make these all the time."

"Who did you make them with?" asked Kyle.

"Oh, my best friend. When we were about your age. Everyone made these in the seventies."

"We make those too," said Kyle. He wasn't wearing any bracelets at the moment, because he kept giving his away to his favorite dogs at the Humane Society, and the dogs couldn't make bracelets for him in return. That didn't seem to bother Kyle. He pulled back Cora's sleeve and showed her six friendship bracelets to Auntie Lake. "See?"

"Everything old is new again," said Auntie Lake, leaning in to look at the bracelets.

"Is she still your best friend?" asked Sybella. "Do you still talk to each other?"

Sybella's question landed in a thorny patch in Cora's heart. Auntie Lake had never told Cora anything about her best friend, and now Sybella was asking about it like she'd known Auntie Lake forever.

Weren't special stories supposed to be saved for the people you were closest to? Cora wanted to go back in time and ask that question before Sybella had a chance to. She wanted Auntie Lake to draw her into a hug and block out everything else and tell her alone the answer.

"No," said Auntie Lake. "We can't talk. Unfortunately she died. Years ago."

"I'm sorry, Auntie Lake," said Kyle, and Sybella added, "Me too."

Cora wanted to say she was sorry too, but she couldn't get the words out, and that made her feel defeated all over again. She couldn't be a good friend. She couldn't even talk about friendship.

Auntie Lake smiled sadly and put the bracelet back, locking the box again and hiding the key. Then she put the box on the shelf and headed for the kitchen.

"Weren't we going to make waffles?" she said, looking back at them. Sybella scrambled to her feet and followed.

"Have you ever made Belgian waffles, Sybella?" Cora heard Auntie Lake ask from the kitchen. "You make them with yeast. Usually I make the dough one day and cook them the next, but I don't think we can wait that long, do you?"

At the word *Belgian,* Cora remembered her mother and how far away she was. Everyone seemed so far away, even people who were in the same room. Or maybe she was just tired. "Never underestimate the power of a nap," her mom liked to say.

Cora's stomach said "waffles" but her heart said

"rest," and after a little argument, her heart won out. "I'm going to my room for a nap," she said. "I mean, our room. I mean, the room."

She ran upstairs and lay on her bed, which was just a bed after all and not a rock in an enchanted river, and closed her eyes.

Auntie Lake's best friend had died. That was so indescribably sad, Cora couldn't think about it for very long. She had never known anyone who had died. People moved, people changed, but dying was different. Even the miles of land and ocean between Berkeley and Belgium weren't the same as the distance between you and someone who had died.

She wanted to ask Auntie Lake more about it, but it felt too scary. Like standing on the edge of a cliff, but instead of feeling inspired, you felt terrified. If the friend had died years ago, she must have been young. Was she still a kid when it happened? That was even scarier.

Cora closed her eyes and watched pictures reel across the darkness. She wasn't sure what a young Auntie Lake would look like. A girl whose face she couldn't quite see, hidden behind a fog. Was that Auntie Lake's friend?

Then, Sybella. Sybella laughing, Sybella leaning in to whisper something, Sybella's serious face when she was thinking. Sybella's sad face.

It was impossible to push pictures out of her mind.

Trying to keep them out only made them rush in, and Cora watched all the pictures of her broken friendship skip past until there were none left.

Eventually she fell asleep.

Cora woke up and went downstairs just as the waffles were being sprinkled with powdered sugar. Sybella divided a box of fresh raspberries between the four plates. "Start with yourself," said Auntie Lake. "You're the guest."

When Sybella got to the last three berries, she put one on her plate, one on Auntie Lake's, and one on Kyle's. There wasn't one left for Cora.

"You can have one of mine," said Kyle, but Cora grabbed her plate before he could give her one of his raspberries, and they ate in silence. Kyle managed to sneak three extra raspberries from his plate to Cora's anyway.

Afterward, the strange mood of the afternoon still hung in the air. They tried a board game, but no one won. Auntie Lake toppled her piece, a bright pink flamingo, and murmured, "The thrill of victory, the agony of defeat."

"What does that mean?" asked Kyle.

"Just something I used to hear on a TV show. A long time ago."

After the board game, they watched Kyle's favorite

show, *Dog Rescue*, but Auntie Lake made them turn it off after three episodes and play charades. "It's your turn to teach me something," she said. "I can't keep up with all the movies and books and singers you like these days, but I'll try to guess."

When it was Kyle's turn, he mimed "Person," and even though he was supposed to use "sounds-like" clues, he mimed juggling. Cora shouted, "Juniper!"

"Is that fair?" said Auntie Lake, and Sybella muttered, "Nothing's fair."

It wasn't *not* fair, exactly. Sybella knew that Juniper juggled. It was only a little unfair for Auntie Lake, but she was a grown-up, and grown-ups weren't supposed to care about winning.

Because she definitely didn't feel like being fair, Cora chose something she thought only Kyle would guess: a book they had picked out from the shelf of books their mom had kept from her own childhood. It was so old that Sybella probably wouldn't have heard of it.

But Sybella, whose mother had a shelf of books from her childhood *and* made Saturdays at the library a regular thing, had heard of every book. Before Cora had mimed *eyes*, Sybella shouted, *"The Girl with the Silver Eyes!"* Kyle had been distracted by his puzzle. Cora glared at him.

"Fine. Your turn," said Cora to Sybella. She very

pointedly looked away from Sybella as they switched places, and then she looked away from Auntie Lake when she saw the unhappy look on her face. She plopped onto the carpet harder than she should have, which she knew hurt no one but herself.

Blip.

Sybella glanced down at her pocket, where her phone was. She hesitated, then took a deep, pre-charades breath and held her hands open, book-style.

Blip.

Blip.

Blip.

"Should you answer that?" asked Auntie Lake. "Is it one of your parents?"

Sybella gave a tight smile and shook her head. "No. That's not their sound."

Blip.

"I'll just . . . hold on." Sybella slid her phone out of her pocket and swiped. "It's just . . . no one." She tried to put her phone back into her pocket, but it slipped out of her fingers and landed screen-up on Auntie Lake's citrus-covered, yellow and orange carpet.

Cora couldn't help it. She leaned forward as Sybella was reaching down, and she saw one word on the screen: MARNIE. Okay, two words, over and over: IT'S MARNIE IT'S MARNIE IT'S MARNIE.

Cora hugged her legs to her chest. Even the San Francisco Bay wasn't big enough to keep Marnie out of her thoughts. Marnie was like ocean plastic: dangerous even when you couldn't see her.

Sybella grabbed her phone and shoved it into her pocket. She looked at Cora, her eyes wide with an emotion Cora couldn't read, and then at Kyle, who quickly said, "Let's keep playing! Come on! You were going to do a book, too, right?"

Sybella nodded. She spread her hands again, then held up two fingers to mean two words, one finger to mean first word, and two fingers again.

"Two," said Kyle. Cora didn't feel like playing along anymore.

"*Two Dogs in a Trench Coat Go to School*!" shouted Kyle. "Oh, wait. That's more than two words."

Second word. Sybella tapped her chin, which she always did when she was thinking. "Chins! *Two Chins*! *Two Faces*!" Kyle shouted.

Sybella shook her head. She pulled on her earlobe for "sounds like," but then she stood still. She tried showing that she was eating something, then that she was reading, doing something else with her hands that Cora couldn't figure out, even if she'd been trying. Sybella made the universal "Come on!" charades face, but no one could guess.

She tried syllables: Tugging her earlobe for "sounds like" and pointing upward, making a surprised face, pointing at herself, but again, everyone was stumped.

"You're going to have to tell us," said Auntie Lake.

Sybella burst out, "*Two Naomis*! Nye-like-sky-oh-me!" She raced through all the gestures again, looking frustrated. "It's only the best book ever."

"I've seen that one in the library!" said Kyle.

"Maybe you should have asked Marnie to play charades with you," said Cora bitterly. She stormed into the kitchen and found a pair of scissors. With a ferocious snap, she cut all her friendship bracelets off, right through the middle, and tossed them into Auntie Lake's kitchen trash can with all the other things that couldn't be used again.

Sybella might have cut hers off too. She might have kept them on, but Cora didn't know. For the rest of the weekend, Sybella kept her sleeves pulled down over her hands and her hands clasped around the cover of the book she was reading about Katherine Johnson and the Space Race.

On Sunday, Auntie Lake drove them all home. She dropped Sybella off at her house first, then drove to the twins' apartment and parked in front.

"Thanks for the great weekend," said Kyle, climbing out of the car.

"Thank you both for coming," said Auntie Lake.

Still in the backseat, Cora leaned forward toward Auntie Lake and said, "It was terrible." She meant it about herself, that *she* was terrible, and maybe Sybella was a little bit terrible, or at least the situation they were in was terrible. But she didn't want Auntie Lake to think she was blaming her, so she added, "I hate everything."

"Do you?" said Auntie Lake, looking back at her. "Everything?"

Cora didn't say it again, but she meant it. Everything.

Cora

After

DR. CLARE WILSON'S VOICEMAIL

Twin Phone

"A lost pet has been reported to the Department of Animal Welfare. It's a dog, and its owner needs it very much. We can't tell you what the dog looks like, or what its name is, or anything else about it, except that it's the best, most loved dog in the world and its owner's name is Kyle. Some people might say that technically it's not even lost, because how can you lose something you've never had? You would think that would be impossible, but it's not. If you find this dog, please return it to its rightful owner. Please."

Speaker Call Back Delete

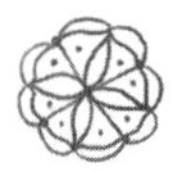

There was garbage in the bathtub again. Cora could identify 1A's scrapbooking scraps and 2B's endless pizza crusts. The guy who lived in 2B seemed to eat nothing but pizza. Pizza minus the crusts.

Two weeks had passed since the terrible weekend at Auntie Lake's, and nothing was back to normal. Friday night used to mean going to Sybella's, or having Sybella over to spend the night. Now it meant watching Dr. Davis sort through all the trash produced by their apartment building in the past week. He called it a Mini Trash-In.

Most Fridays since March had been bad—most *days* had been bad, really—but this Friday, their eleventh birthday, was the worst. It had started badly when there was no video call from their mom before breakfast, and she hadn't picked up when Cora and Kyle had tried calling her. Then they'd had to walk past the Toad, knowing that Sybella wouldn't be waiting to rub its head for extra birthday luck. Sybella had just gone into school like it was any other day, as if she didn't care that it was Cora and Kyle's birthday, or even that it was her own birthday. The day hadn't gotten any better after that. Even the thought of a special birthday dinner couldn't cheer Cora up.

She stared into the tub. Their neighbors didn't seem to be paying attention to the signs she and Kyle had made on a Friday night a couple weeks ago and hung up on both floors of their building:

What's in Your Garbage?

Toss It or Recycle It?

Compost Does a Planet Good!

Don't Throw It All Away!

They had drawn pictures of cans, bottles, newspapers, food scraps, cereal boxes, and more, and arrows pointing to green garbage cans, brown compost buckets, and blue recycling cans. A can for everything and everything in its can, as Dr. Davis said.

They'd even helped make a worm box for all the food scraps, but that didn't stop 2B and his crusts.

Dr. Davis expertly sorted everything into piles and

put each pile into a small can of the right color. Later, he would take it all outside to the big cans to be picked up by the city trucks. "Well, that's it for the neighbors' trash. What about you two?"

Dr. Davis's goal for their home was zero waste, meaning that they could recycle or compost everything and didn't send anything to the landfill, but that didn't happen every week.

Cora and Kyle brought out the little garbage cans from their rooms, made from folded and woven strips of recycled paper, and held them upside down—nothing. Not a scrap fell out, and Dr. Davis smiled. "Nothing in your pockets? Nothing up your sleeves?" he asked, like they were magicians.

Kyle's jean pockets were empty. Cora reached into hers and found an old waxed paper bag from a bakery, the kind that was just big enough to hold one cookie or one scone.

"Ah, waxed paper," said Dr. Davis. "Where does that go?"

Cora wondered what Sybella was doing. Probably something fun and birthday-ish. Probably not sorting garbage. Then she wondered if she was supposed to wonder about it or if she wasn't supposed to care anymore.

"With food waste for composting!" said Kyle.

"Right!" said Dr. Davis. He opened the food waste can, and Cora tossed the bag in. "Why don't you two get ready for dinner? We'll walk to McGinnis's when Lake gets here."

"McGinnis's!" said Kyle. "Chocolate lava cake!"

"Are we spending the night with her?" asked Cora.

"Tomorrow's the Trashlympics!" said Kyle. "We can't miss that!"

Of course they couldn't. Cora had almost forgotten, even though Dani had reminded them at the Trash Team meeting yesterday.

"Next weekend?" she asked.

"That's the art contest," said Dr. Davis. "Have you been working on your project?"

"I need to get dressed," said Cora. "I don't want to be late for dinner."

She scrambled into her room before Dr. Davis could ask any follow-up questions about her art project, which she had not been working on.

She changed into the best leggings she owned, light blue ones made of organic cotton and covered in tiny ice cream cones, and grabbed a hoodie to go over her shirt. Then Kyle knocked on her door.

"It's Mom!"

Kyle had put on his only suit jacket right over his T-shirt and jeans. He'd found the jacket weeks ago while he was sorting garbage in the building's basement with Dr. Davis.

Cora looked at the wind-up clock on her nightstand. If it was six o'clock in Berkeley, then it was three in the morning in Belgium. What was her mother doing awake at three o'clock in the morning? She opened the door, and Kyle held out the Twin Phone so they could both see Dr. Wilson's face. "It's the middle of the night!" said Cora.

"Happy birthday!" said Dr. Wilson. She yawned. "I'm sorry about this morning. Our network went down. But I couldn't let your birthday pass without calling. I woke up just for this."

"Auntie Lake is coming," said Kyle. "We're going to McGinnis's."

"Save me a bite of chocolate lava cake," said Dr. Wilson. She gave a little smile.

Cora wanted to ask her if she'd thought enough about the future and if she could come home now, but she knew it wouldn't be that easy. Why two people who loved the same thing couldn't love each other enough to stay together was a mystery to Cora. Watching her parents split up last year had been like watching a trash-tracking simulation: The movement started at a red dot, the center point, and red lines spread outward from there, separating as the pieces of trash left the city and went on their own journeys, never to reunite.

Her mother had said she'd only be away for a year, that she would be back in July, but Cora had tracked a lot of things that had been thrown away. She knew that just because you could tell where something was and where it had been didn't mean it was going to come back.

"Did my present get there in time?"

"No," said Cora. "What is it?" Cora hated to wait for surprises. Kyle, on the other hand, was endlessly patient—and optimistic.

"It'll probably be here tomorrow," Kyle said before their mom could reply. "We'll look for it in the mail. Or maybe we got one of those little notes saying we have to pick it up at the post office."

Cora could see that he was trying to let their mother know it was all right that her present wasn't there, that she wasn't there. But it wasn't all right. It wasn't just that Cora wanted the present, although she did. The present, whatever it was, would be something to connect Cora to her mom across all that space, like the lines on the map. Only instead of moving away, like everything else, it would be moving toward her.

"I won't keep you from your birthday dinner," said Dr. Wilson. "I just had to call. And now I have to sleep. Talk to you soon?"

There was more that Cora wanted to say. She'd told her mom a little about the problems she was having with

Sybella, but without her mom right there, it was hard to get the story right. It sounded stupid and embarrassing when she went over it in her head. Leaving public service announcements when she knew her mom wouldn't be able to answer the phone was easier.

"Yeah, Mom," said Kyle. "Talk to you soon."

"I'll save you some cake," said Cora. "Not really."

Dr. Wilson laughed. "I love you both," she said, and they ended the call. Kyle stared at the blank screen and blinked as if he might cry. Cora threw her arms around him because she felt as if *she* might cry, and although they were both very good at crying, this time, for some reason, they didn't.

After a minute, Kyle was cheerful again. He held up the phone. "I put a new game on here. It's called *SuperVet.* You have to figure out what's wrong with people's pets and help them get better. Do you want to play?"

That was the most Kyle-sounding game Cora had ever heard of. It was not the game for her.

"I'm going to see if Auntie Lake's here yet," said Cora. She kept watch from the living room window. As soon as she saw Auntie Lake's car, she shouted to Kyle, and they ran downstairs to meet her before she could ring the doorbell to their apartment.

Cora hugged Auntie Lake and then held her hand. "I'm glad you came," she said.

Auntie Lake gave Cora's hand a squeeze. "I know your mom wishes she could be here," she said.

"Why does it take a year to think about the future?" asked Cora. She kicked at an empty snail shell that lay next to the front steps. "Being grown up is like . . . *living* in the future. Why does she even have to think about it?"

"It's the most important things that take the most time," said Auntie Lake.

Cora wasn't sure about that. If something was that important, wouldn't the answer be obvious?

"But it's a lovely evening, and it's your birthday!" said Auntie Lake. "Let's remember that. Tell me something good that happened today."

Nothing good had happened besides the call from Dr. Wilson, but Cora decided to rein in her grumpiness, if only for a while. She told Auntie Lake about the herbs she'd picked from the school garden that morning for the cafeteria staff, one of Ms. Nuñez's many hands-on lessons about sustainability, and pointed out her favorite rosemary bush in the patch that grew in front of her apartment. They both touched it and held their fingers to their noses. Auntie Lake identified other plants for Cora—sages, lupines, honeysuckle, and goldenrod. When Dr. Davis joined them, wearing a clean shirt and carrying a garbage bag, they started walking.

"Don't tell me you're going to pick up trash on the

way to your children's birthday dinner," said Auntie Lake.

"Never miss an opportunity," said Dr. Davis, although Cora could tell that the bag was already full. Presents! As practical as her dad was most of the time, every once in a while he did something fun, and bringing presents to dinner to open over chocolate lava cake was fun. Plus he'd get to educate the restaurant on how to properly dispose of the wrapping paper.

Usually walking anywhere with her family took a little longer than it should have, because Dr. Davis stopped to pick up crumpled paper cups and food wrappers with his plastic extendable trash grippers and put it all in a black garbage bag, and Kyle stopped to admire every dog they saw. Tonight they were still slow, not because of picking up trash, but because Auntie Lake stopped to exclaim over how much things had changed since she had lived in Berkeley as a child.

They passed Cora's favorite café, Au Coquelet, on the way. Sometimes they went there on Saturday mornings for a cookie or a piece of pie, but not often. Today, a teenage girl was sitting on the sidewalk near the door, holding a cup with a few coins at the bottom. She was wearing a worn black leather jacket and staring down at her boots.

There were always street kids downtown, sitting

in front of stores or huddled between buildings. The streets were filled with homeless adults too, but it was always the young ones who made Cora feel the worst. This girl was maybe eighteen or nineteen, an adult but not really grown up. Cora couldn't tell. Then she looked away, because she knew she wasn't supposed to stare.

Kyle kneeled down to greet a Goldendoodle that was tied to a bike rack, and Dr. Davis and Auntie Lake talked about which businesses were new and which had been there forever and which ones they missed the most. Cora glanced at the girl and remembered that she had put a raspberry fruit leather, which she had earned from Ms. Nuñez for all her help in the garden, into the pocket of her hoodie in case she got hungry on the way to dinner. She offered it to the girl, not sure if she should say anything, and eventually the girl looked up. She took the fruit leather and looked it over. "Hey, thanks," she said, but she didn't smile.

The girl looked down at her feet again, and Cora moved awkwardly away.

When they got to McGinnis's, Kyle paused outside the door. "Birthday Booth?" he said to Cora.

Cora grinned. "Yeah!" The Birthday Booth wasn't only for people having birthdays, but they'd sat in it for their tenth birthday last year and decided that they would sit there for every birthday if they could. It was the best booth, close to the little stage where people sometimes played the fiddle or sang, but not too close. The red upholstery on the seats wasn't torn (much), and there was a poster above the booth that showed someone chasing a seal with a glass on its nose. On their last birthday, Sybella had looked at the poster and said—but it didn't matter what Sybella had said. Not anymore.

"You have to see the Birthday Booth, Auntie Lake," said Cora, pulling a little on Auntie Lake's hand.

"I don't think I have a choice," said Auntie Lake.

Cora swung the door open wide and took a step toward the Birthday Booth. Then she saw who was sitting there. Digging her fork into chocolate lava cake and laughing with her parents. Because it was her birthday too, after all.

Sybella looked at Cora, then at her cake, then up at the ceiling. Cora wanted to glare at Sybella, but she didn't. For one thing, she wasn't very confrontational. But more than that, she remembered something Sybella had said once, that even here, in California, people sometimes stared when she went out with her parents. They stared at her father, who was white, and at her mother, who was black, and looked puzzled, or suspicious, or something else. That did still matter, even if she and Sybella were fighting. So Cora didn't glare at them, because even though she suddenly felt grumpy again, she didn't want to be one of those people.

"Isn't that—" Auntie Lake started to say when Kyle, whose timing was flawless, grabbed Cora's other hand and dragged her toward the worst booth in McGinnis's, saying, "Look! The Birthday Booth is free!"

It was not the Birthday Booth. It should have been called the Bathroom Booth, since it was right next to the bathrooms. Its upholstery was torn on both sides, a post blocked the view of the stage, and the poster above it showed a glass of beer with a creepy smiley face in its foam. The only good thing about it was that once Cora slid into the seat next to Kyle, she could no longer see Sybella and her parents.

She stared at the post.

"Well," said Auntie Lake, "this is a . . . very nice booth."

It wasn't, but Cora knew that she and Kyle would keep pretending that this was really where they had wanted to sit and that nothing at all was wrong.

"I'm glad they use sustainably harvested Alaskan cod in the fish and chips here," said Dr. Davis, trying to be conversational. "The collapse of the Atlantic northwest cod fishery—"

"Dad!" said Kyle. "Can we have our presents?"

Normally Kyle would cheerfully have listened to their dad's lecture on collapsed fisheries or resource streams or any of the other things he liked to talk about, but because Kyle was the best twin, he must have seen that Cora needed to be distracted by something other than fish.

"Presents?" said Dr. Davis. "Don't we usually open presents after dinner?"

"I thought we could play the guessing game," said Kyle. "You know, let us shake the packages and guess what's inside."

"Well, if it involves you two using the evidence of your senses combined with past experience to make educated guesses, I'm all for it," said Dr. Davis. In other words, yes.

"You always did know how to have fun, Duncan," said Auntie Lake.

A waiter took their order—four plates of sustainably harvested Alaskan cod and chips, with a side of steamed seasonal vegetables for Dr. Davis. While they waited, Kyle and Cora poked, shook, and even sniffed their birthday packages, which were wrapped, as always, in previously used brown paper grocery bags. Both packages were large and square, but the twins knew, from past experience, not to assume that large gifts were always the best.

"A loom?" guessed Kyle. "Based on my past experience of you giving me a sheep's fleece and a spinning wheel for Christmas?"

"Mine is a Stellar Suzy Glam n' Jam Home Nail Salon," said Cora, although she knew it wasn't. No pink-plastic-cased tote of toxic beauty supplies would ever enter Dr. Davis's shopping cart, or his home, or Cora's life. Not that she really wanted one. She agreed with most of the eco-friendly rules her parents set, but sometimes, *sometimes,* she wished she could have what other kids had, do what other kids did, and forget that everything she touched was one day going to turn into garbage. She sighed. "Based on my past experience of you giving me a subscription to the Whole Grain of the Month Club for Christmas."

"You didn't," said Auntie Lake to Dr. Davis. "No. You wouldn't. Did you?"

"Never underestimate the importance of early lessons in nutrition," replied Dr. Davis. Cora thought she saw his cheeks turn slightly red.

"I got barley last month," said Cora.

"Ridiculous," said Auntie Lake. "Based on *my* past experiences as a child whose mother tried to make her eat barley, I think I ought to give you both your presents immediately." She rummaged in her bag and brought out two small packages. They were wrapped in brown paper too, because Auntie Lake also believed in reusing and recycling, but she had taken the time to draw things on them: dogs for Kyle and a mermaid for Cora.

Kyle's gift was a tiny porcelain Labrador and a gift certificate for the Berkeley Humane Society.

Kyle seemed to glow. He had wanted a dog for years, a dog he could never have because dogs weren't allowed in their building. But Cora could practically see a light inside him that blazed when he thought about dogs, when he washed dogs, when he petted dogs in the park.

That flame had burned a little brighter this past year, when their apartment was emptier without their mom, and their hearts didn't know where to send all that extra love. Belgium, obviously, but Belgium was thousands of miles away, and Cora didn't know if love could make it that far without thinning out, like dough stretched out between your hands.

"I know your landlord has some silly rule against dogs, but I also know that sometimes you need something to hope for. This will cover the adoption fees for a senior dog, when the time comes," said Auntie Lake. "A senior is one that's—"

"More than seven years old, I know!" said Kyle. "One of my favorites is a senior. His name is Sir Walter Dog! Thank you! Thank you!" said Kyle. "Dad, do you remember Sir Walter Dog? I mean, I know we can't have a dog. But maybe Mrs. Pruitt will change her mind if it's the right dog?"

"Unfortunately, 'no dogs' is inclusive of all dogs, Kyle. There is no dog that falls outside the parameter of 'no dogs,' by definition. If it did, it wouldn't be a dog."

"What does that mean?" Cora asked for Kyle, since she knew he would politely pretend that he understood what their father was talking about.

"It means, no dogs."

"Perhaps we need to talk to this landlord," said Auntie Lake.

Dr. Davis shook his head. "Don't go trying to work your magic on Mrs. Pruitt, Lake. You'll just get Kyle's hopes up. And besides, the amount of waste produced each year by the average pet dog—"

"Too late!" said Kyle. "My hopes are already up!" He bounced in his seat to prove it. "Open yours, Cora!"

Cora unwrapped her present. Like Kyle, she got a porcelain figure—a small mermaid. "It reminded me of you," said Auntie Lake.

The porcelain mermaid was nice and round, which was how Cora thought of herself, but other than that, she couldn't see anything that was the same. The mermaid had red hair, and Cora had brown hair. The mermaid had a tail, and obviously Cora didn't. It looked sort of surprised and mournful at the same time, its red lips making an *O* and its eyes plastered open. Cora hoped that wasn't how she looked.

"Mermaids are adventurers too," Auntie Lake said. "And dreamers. Like you."

Was she really an adventurer? Or a dreamer? Cora wasn't sure about either.

Tucked inside the box was a gift certificate, but this one was handwritten. On the line where the amount should have been, Auntie Lake had written: *Good for the thing you need the most. Expires: never.*

"Thank you," Cora said. But how could a piece of paper give her what she needed the most? Did Auntie Lake's gift certificate have the power to bring her mother all the way back from Belgium? Or send Cora into the past, to before she had lost her best friend?

The waiter came with their dinners. Tangled in her thoughts, Cora slumped down in her seat, which made her foot stick out from underneath the table, which made the waiter holding the four plates of fish and chips stumble, which sent the fish and chips tumbling into the air and then down, down, down onto the table, and Dr. Davis's lap, and Cora's head.

As Cora picked fries out of her hair, Sybella passed their booth on her way to the bathroom. It was obvious that she was looking at Cora but pretending not to, because who wouldn't look at someone who shared a birthday with you, who had once been your friend, and who was now picking fries out of her hair?

On the way back, Sybella stopped at their table long enough to drop something on the table in front of Cora, then she ran back to her booth. It was a friendship bracelet, one of the ones Sybella had made for their centennial. And it had been cut in half.

Kyle put his hand on Cora's arm, and Auntie Lake murmured, "Everything old . . ."

After that, Cora barely tasted the fish and chips brought out to replace the ones that had ended up all over her. She didn't blow out the candle on her chocolate lava cake, pulling it up like a weed instead and dousing it in her milk. She stabbed at her cake and tore open her present from Dr. Davis—a loom, to foster collaboration with Kyle, who had received more wool.

Dr. Davis brought one more package out of the black garbage bag. "From your mother," he said, a little stiffly. Cora's stabbiness dwindled then, seeing that her mother's present had made it in time after all, and that her dad had brought it along to be part of the occasion.

Dr. Wilson had sent them both 3D puzzles of Belgian landmarks and four boxes of seashell-shaped chocolates. She sent them chocolates every month or so, but never four boxes at once. The card read, "I love you enough for a hundred boxes of chocolates, but I could only fit four in the package. Happy birthday! Love, Mom."

In a silent agreement, Kyle took both of the puzzles and one box of chocolates, leaving Cora with three. She found one last fry in her hair, ate it, and they left. Sybella and her parents had already gone. Cora, covered in fries and humiliation, hadn't noticed them leave.

A block away from McGinnis's, they ran into Dani. Cora was about to introduce her to Auntie Lake when Auntie Lake reached out and gave Dani a hug.

"You know each other?" asked Cora.

"Yes," said Auntie Lake, but before she could explain how, Kyle tugged on her arm and held out the Twin Phone, where he had used some of their precious data to pull up pictures of Sir Walter Dog.

"He's a West Highland terrier. There's also Cauliflower. She's a hound mix. I think I like big dogs more than small dogs. But a small dog takes up less space, and our apartment is small. But big dogs can be calm, and small dogs can be kind of jumpy. What do you think?"

Kyle and Auntie Lake scrolled through dogs together, while Dr. Davis inspected the garbage can on the corner and Dani picked another fry from Cora's hood.

"Is there a story here?"

"Probably," said Cora, eating the fry. Then the whole thing came out, faster than she meant it to, about what had happened with Sybella, the things she'd said and the things she hadn't said, and how she felt like a traitor to her friend but also a little like she'd been betrayed.

"Was it so bad, though?" asked Dani. "It sounds like maybe it's just a misunderstanding. Do you want me to talk to her?"

"No!" She didn't need grown-ups fixing her problems for her like she was a preschooler, even if Dani barely counted as a grown-up.

"So you're just going to suffer?" asked Dani.

"Yes?"

"Look, everyone has friend problems at your age. It's a fact. I hated my best friend Anna for about three weeks in sixth grade."

"Was she your girlfriend?" Cora tried to picture a Dani who was her own age, but it was hard to imagine her without the tattoos.

"You're so nosy!" Dani laughed. "I didn't have a girlfriend until I was in high school. This was just a friend."

"What did she do?"

"She ruined a painting I was working on. She was goofing around and knocked into it, and it broke the frame I was making and tore the paper. I was *so* mad.

And you know what? I didn't even like the painting. I hated it, but I had to work on it because it was for a class project. Now I wish I'd been a little more chill. A little more understanding."

"I don't know how to be chill," said Cora. "I only know how to be me."

"Truth," said Dani. "But it's not too late. She's not gone forever. You're not gone forever."

That made Cora think of Auntie Lake's friend, the one who had died. "But I feel like she threw me away! Like when you throw out stuff you don't want anymore. People are always throwing out stuff when they don't know what to do with it, and they don't care where it ends up. It's the same with people. You can't even recycle people. You could sort them, like you sort trash, and make a pile for the people you want and a pile for the people you don't want. But that's it. There's no blue bin for people. You just use them up and throw them away." She could feel the tears coming. "Why do people throw other people away? I hate that. I hate it. It isn't fair."

"Definitely not chill," said Dani, putting an arm around Cora. Then her phone beeped.

She pulled it out of her pocket. "No way." She tapped the screen. "No way."

Beep-beep.

Cora wiped her eyes on her sleeve. "What?"

Dani didn't answer. Her eyes went from her phone to the street, up and down the sidewalk, and across to the other side.

Beep-beep-beep.

"Where are you?" Dani muttered. "Come on, I know you're here somewhere."

Cora got a glimpse of Dani's screen, and she recognized TrashTrack. "Are we tracking something? Is there trash up here?"

Which was a silly thing to ask. Cora knew what her dad would say: "There's trash everywhere." In fact, he had said exactly that one time, followed by, "That means there's opportunity everywhere." And Juniper, who had been there too, had said, "Trash-itunity!"

Dani scanned the street for the trash-itunity, whatever it was. People were everywhere, and a few pieces of trash blew along in the breeze, but none of them seemed to be what Dani was looking for.

"Remember that boot we started tracking at the beginning of the school year?" she said.

"Yeah?"

Cora remembered the tracker Dani had put on the boot as a demonstration at the first Trash Team meeting. The signal had died after a couple of days.

"It must have been a faulty device," said Dani. "When the signal died, the boot was still in my truck.

I didn't even get it into the waste stream, so I just pulled it out of the collection bag. I was going to take it back to the lab to see if I could get the tracker working again, but I guess I dropped it somewhere on the way, or it fell out of my truck. But now it's back, and it's near here somewhere. And it's moving. I can't believe the battery's still working."

"Is someone carrying it?" asked Cora.

"Or wearing it."

Dani kept her eyes low, looking at the feet of everyone passing by. Cora looked too, wondering why a boot would be put in the trash and taken out again, and if it was the same person who had done both, and if it was because that someone had found its match.

She saw a pair of boots heading up the street. She couldn't remember exactly what the boot had looked like, but she thought it had been like these, black, and tall enough to go halfway up someone's calf. The boots coming toward them were black, but one looked more worn than the other, and its laces were frayed at the ends. The tongue flopped down, and the sole flapped open at the toe.

The boots came closer, and Cora saw their person between all the other bodies on the street, in a black leather jacket with her dark brown hair stuck up from her head in short spikes. It was the girl she'd given her fruit leather to on the way to McGinnis's, but the girl didn't seem to notice Cora. She probably saw hundreds of people walking by every day, so why would she remember any of them, even the ones who stopped to give her fruit leather?

Dani saw her too, but she didn't say anything. They watched the girl walk slowly past them. Dani looked down at the boot and up at the girl's face as if she were trying to work something out.

"That's the boot, right?" asked Cora after she had passed. "Do you know that girl?"

"Yes," said Dani. "No. That's the boot. I don't know the girl."

"At least you found it!" said Cora. "You thought it was gone, but it walked right up to you. That's a pretty good story."

"Yeah," said Dani. "That is a good story."

Cora

After

DR. CLARE WILSON'S VOICEMAIL

Twin Phone

"It has come to our attention that people are getting a little confused about how to sort their trash. Here's a refresher from Cora, Queen of Recycling: If something is gross and it hurts your feelings, you should probably throw it away. If it reminds you of something you used to enjoy, or someone you used to like, put it in a different pile so you can think about it later. If it contains the story of your life and all the most important things about you, keep it. Why would you ever throw the story of your life away?"

Speaker Call Back Delete

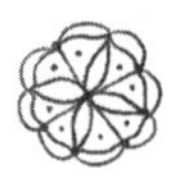

Early the next morning, Cora woke to marching band music. It happened every time Dr. Davis was particularly excited about something, and this morning he was excited about the Trashlympics. The sound of drums and sousaphones filled their apartment, and Dr. Davis marched along as he made breakfast. It was another one of his ideas of fun.

Cora had to admit that Trashlympics breakfast was better than normal breakfast. She walked to the kitchen—walked, not marched—and met Kyle coming out of his bedroom, swinging his arms like he was in a parade. Dr. Davis had poured unfiltered apple juice into three glasses and was drizzling local wildflower honey onto slabs of cinnamon-raisin French toast.

"Ready for the best day of the year?" he asked. Kyle shouted, "Yes!" and played an imaginary bugle. Cora stuck her finger into her French toast and dug out a raisin.

As far as Cora was concerned, the only good thing about the Trashlympics was that Dani would be there. If she stuck close to Dani the whole time and offered to help, she might not have to actually participate. Her whole life was a festival of recycling. She should already have a million trash points, so why should she have to do the Trashlympics too?

But when they got to the gym, Dani wasn't there.

"She'll be here later," said Juniper. Today he was wearing a T-shirt that said *Earth Day 3019: Let's Hope We Get There.* "Something came up."

Cora plopped down onto a bench to wait, but Kyle pulled her to her feet. "Help me make signs," he said, handing her a thick black marker and a cardboard box. Juniper helped them cut the sides of the box to use as poster board, and they made signs for the registration table and for each of the events around the gym.

Every time Cora tried to sit down, Kyle found something else for her to do, until it was nine o'clock and kids from elementary schools all over the district started trickling in to register.

"One more sign," said Kyle. "Can you put this on

the main door?" He handed Cora his *Welcome to the Trashlympics* sign. Cora had wanted to make a sign that said *Welcome to the Most Garbage Day of Your Life*, but Dr. Davis had voted no.

Kyle, who was earning extra trash points as an event volunteer, started giving out number bibs and showing participants where to go.

Cora trudged down the hall to the main door. She pulled it open, and in twirled Marnie Stoll.

"Oh, hi, Cora," she sang. Then, clinging to the doorframe, she leaned out and shouted, "Come on, we'll be late!"

Cora looked past her and saw Sybella lugging a trash bag across the parking lot, and her dad following along behind. She didn't know if Sybella had seen her, but she dropped the *Welcome* sign and ran back to the gym, climbing to the top of the bleachers, as high up and invisible as she could get.

Dani still hadn't turned up. Cora remembered what Dani had said the night before—that maybe Cora's problems with Sybella were all just a misunderstanding. That was true, but it wasn't the point. Someone could hate you just as much for a misunderstanding, and it was just as hard to make things right.

Marnie made her way to the registration table, and her extra-loud voice bounced around the gym. "Of course

I have a team! You know who is on my team? Sybella. Sybella Seward is on my team."

Sybella, wearing a pair of red gloves, was looking through the trash she'd brought. She lifted her head at the sound of her name, but she was facing away from Cora, so Cora couldn't see her expression.

Of course she was on Marnie's team. Of course. She was probably smiling.

Miraculously, Dr. Davis was so busy announcing and refereeing that he didn't seem to notice Cora sitting on the sidelines.

Her invisibility was working.

She watched the Trash-In, where everyone sorted the things they had brought from home into piles of recyclables and a pile destined for the landfill. College student volunteers weighed everything and tallied the results, which were shown as a chart on a giant screen at the end of the gym.

Some teams had made T-shirts with names like Trash Monsters and Garbanimals. Sybella and Marnie didn't have shirts, but they were each wearing one of the red gloves. They fist-bumped with their red-gloved hands, and Cora's heart went *thud.*

She did *not* pay attention to how many trash points Sybella was earning. It was too many to count, anyway, because Sybella threw herself into everything she did, from exploring the playground to sorting trash. During the trash-and-field events, Cora tried not to watch as Sybella dashed and Marnie stumbled in the relay race (the Trash and Dash), where instead of handing off the water bottle batons, they dropped them into a bin and grabbed a new one for their partner to run with.

Kyle hadn't found a new team, but now he joined a couple of other lone trashletes and raced next to Sybella and Marnie. Sybella's team came in first and Kyle's came in second, and Cora grumbled, then cheered.

Just before Capture the Trash began, Dani finally arrived and tossed her bag near the bleachers. "Aren't you going to join in?" she called up to Cora, and although Cora didn't want to join in, she was relieved that she wasn't invisible to Dani.

"Do I have to?"

Dani pretended to think, tilting her head toward the ceiling. "Yes."

"But I don't have a team."

"You can be an alternate. Come on." She grabbed a number bib for Cora from the registration table. "Here, you're number seventy-four."

Cora tied her bib on, and Dani started handing out flags made of fabric scraps for Capture the Trash.

"Volunteers, can I get all the extra bags of recyclables over here at center court? Just dump it all out. We'll have four teams play at a time. Each team should have three to four people. Teams, the objective of Capture the Trash is to gather different types of recyclables and trash from the circle, one at a time, and bring them to the bins in your quadrant of the court." She pointed to the bins that were being set up around the perimeter of the basketball court. "You have bins for mixed paper, corrugated cardboard, aluminum, other metals, electronic waste, food waste, and plastics. Remember, only some plastics can be recycled—bottles and rigid containers, no straws, no candy wrappers or chip bags. Any questions?"

"Is there really glass in that pile?" asked a parent.

"And food waste?" asked another, looking worried.

"No. In this game we're substituting these blue cards for glass and these green cards for food waste." Dani held up blue and green index cards. "They're marked too, so all the blue cards have *glass* on them and the green cards say *food waste*. Got it?"

Everyone nodded.

"You can have two runners at a time on the court and one or two to switch out when your runners get their flags pulled. Your flags cannot be pulled while you're in the center circle or after you've reached your safety zone. Each runner has two flags, and when both flags have been pulled, that runner is out until someone else on the team gets out. Collect your flags and give them to the next person on your team. You must also take any items that runner collected during their time on the court out of your collection bins and return them to center court. The first team to get ten items in the correct bins wins. You'll need at least one thing in each category."

As the volunteers dumped trash at center court, four teams stepped up to compete, tying on their flag belts and huddling up to talk about how to separate recyclable materials and trash. Marnie had found a third team member, a nervous-looking girl Cora didn't recognize, to play with her and Sybella.

Cora looked for Kyle, hoping he would join her on the sidelines, but he was facing away from her and seemed to be explaining the rules to a group of younger kids. And even though he was the best twin, he probably wouldn't want to give up his chance to earn more trash points.

Dani blew the whistle. "Go, trashletes!"

Sybella and Marnie ran toward the trash pile, their striped flags flapping. Sybella took a root beer can, and Marnie took a paper plate. Sybella made it to the safety zone with her can and tossed it into the bin, but Marnie hesitated too long and another team's runner snatched one of her flags. She turned to complain instead of running for safety, and her other flag was gone.

The nervous girl tied Marnie's flag belt around her

waist and went in. She tiptoed toward the trash pile, flinching as runners swerved toward her, and reached for a paper napkin. She turned to run back and froze. She was still inside the center circle, safe from flag-pulling, and apparently she was happy to stay that way.

"Run!" shouted Sybella, grabbing a ball of aluminum foil. "Go on!"

Marnie yelled from the safety zone, but the girl wouldn't move. Marnie's pale face got redder and redder as the other teams collected items. Cora didn't know if she wanted the girl to move or not. She didn't want her to be scared, but it was sort of fun to watch Marnie get angry.

Sybella collected two more items and was expertly dodging the other runners. She dropped a plastic fork in the garbage bin and stepped into the safety zone to catch her breath. With sparks shooting out of her eyes, Marnie charged onto the court, heading for the center.

Was she going to rip the napkin out of the girl's hand? Take her belt and toss her to the side?

"Hey!" called Dani, pointing at Marnie. "Number thirteen! You're not wearing flags! Get back to your safety zone!"

Marnie would not listen. She barreled toward the girl, who was still frozen and looked even frozener now that she was about to be run over. At the last minute, she jumped, letting Marnie run head-on into the pile of trash.

"Ahhhh!" The cry came not from Marnie, who was too surprised to say anything and sat amongst plastics, mixed paper, and soda cans with her mouth hanging open. It came instead from the target of Marnie's wrath, who had twisted her ankle in her leap to avoid being tackled.

After Juniper, who was a volunteer first responder, checked the girl's ankle and made sure it wasn't broken, he and Dani helped her to the bleachers. Juniper went for the first aid kit, and Dani waved to Cora. "Your turn, alternate." She grinned and offered a flag belt to Cora. "You lost twenty trash points, number thirteen," she said to Marnie.

"Go, Cora!" called Kyle from the other end of the court.

Everything moved very slowly after that, except the parts that moved too fast. Cora slogged onto the court, dragged herself to the pile, reached through Jell-O to pick up a sour cream container. Or at least that's how it felt.

Sybella skimmed over the court. She needed no alternate, she was a team unto herself. She was first to the safety zone, just like she had always been first at everything. First to learn to multiply double-digit numbers. First to walk across the top of the playground bars like a tightrope walker. First to get a double smiley face on a school project, her Farmers' Market Math poster. Okay, the only one to get a double smiley face on a school project. Cora was not generally up to double smiley face work.

It had been fun to have a friend who was good at everything but who never made you feel bad that you weren't. A little of that glamour had rubbed off onto non-glamorous Cora, and for a while kids had treated her as if she were a star too. *Sybella and Cora. Cora and Sybella. They'll do anything.* When really it was only Sybella who would do anything, and Cora who would share her chocolate milk with Sybella afterward. Sybella could have shared anyone's chocolate milk—a dozen other kids would have gladly given theirs to the brave explorer of the playground bars—but she always sat with Cora because that's what best friends did. "*Aquafaba patria est,*" they'd said as they passed the milk carton between them.

Now, as she watched Sybella go for her ninth piece of trash, something stirred in Cora. Not anger, exactly. Not envy. She wanted, after all this time, to prove that she was someone who had been worth being friends with. And the only way she could think to do that was to be better than Sybella at something. Just once.

Her whole body woke up. Cora flew toward the trash pile, looking for something to go in the landfill bin. At the top of the pile she saw something reddish, a book with duct tape on its spine. Trash! Hardcover books couldn't be recycled unless you removed the cover, and the duct tape wasn't recyclable either. She reached for it at the same time that another hand grabbed it and started to pull.

Cora held on with both hands, and Sybella yanked it toward her. The book fell open, and each girl held tight to one side. "What are you doing?" grunted Sybella. "We're on. The same. Team."

"I need to put this in the landfill bin," said Cora.

"It's paper! It goes in the recycling!" said Sybella.

"Landfill!"

"Recycling!"

They pulled the book back and forth like they were playing tug-of-war. But Cora knew this wasn't a game. She gave one final, mighty tug—and the duct tape tore off, splitting the book in two and sending Cora and Sybella sprawling to the floor, each clutching half.

It hadn't mattered in the end where the red book should have gone, because Kyle's team collected their tenth item, and just as Cora and Sybella hit the floor, Dani blew the whistle. The game was over. Cora and Sybella looked at each other and thought exactly the same thing, as they had so many times before, when they were still friends. This time, the thought was: *Run away!*

Sybella ran to her dad in the bleachers, and Cora ran into one of the locker rooms, where she stayed until she heard people streaming out of the gym, and she guessed that the Trashlympics were over.

It turned out that Sybella hadn't been first at everything. A tear dribbled down Cora's cheek. She, Cora, had always been the first to cry.

"Center yourself," Dr. Wilson always told her when she got upset. "Let calmness flow gently down to your fingers and toes." While Cora was trying to force calmness to flow down to her fingers and toes, she realized that she still had the torn book in her hand. It was a diary, the kind that came with a tiny, cheap lock that opened with a tiny, cheap key. But there was no need to unlock it now, because all that was left of the lock was the piece on the front cover. Sybella's half must have had the strap and the other piece of the lock.

Who left a diary unlocked, to be ripped apart by fighting trashletes? And who put their diary in the trash to begin with? Dr. Davis had told them that once someone threw something away, legally it didn't belong to them anymore. So Cora didn't feel too bad about opening the diary to the first page. The handwriting was like her own, a loopy, messy scrawl.

April 20, 1974

My life is garbage.

Cora could sympathize with that, and she settled back against a locker to read.

From the Diary of
Penny Ellen Chambord

April 20, 1974

My life is garbage. Lulu is being ridiculous. I am not a spy. Why did she have to tell everyone that I am? And now everyone hates me. I hate her. She's an awful, awful human being. Lulu=Not My Best Friend Anymore.

By the way, thank you, Lulu, for giving me this diary as an early birthday present. It was a very kind present, and I'm sorry I'll never be able to thank you properly since we are no longer friends.

I suppose I should write down what happened in all its grisly detail because this diary is a historical document like the Watergate tapes that President Nixon made. I don't have tapes, but I will write it down because I want people to know the truth.

The thing is, anyone can start a school club if they get twenty signatures and a teacher to be the sponsor. I told Lulu we should start an Earth Club, because there is only one Earth and we need to take care of it. She agreed.

I had twenty signatures, and Miss Meacham was going to be the sponsor. By the way, she says she's definitely Miss Meacham and not Ms. Meacham, whatever that means. A club needs a secretary, so Lulu said she would be the secretary. A club also needs a president, and I said I would be the president because it was my idea and I have leadership qualifications. I was dodgeball captain twice this year in gym, and everyone else was only captain once.

Lulu said she thought that would be okay, but then along came Violet Dixon, saying that she wanted to be president too, and there should be an election. "That's what democracy is," she said, and I said, "I know all about democracy because I watch the nightly news. Even presidents can get themselves in a lot of hot water."

I bet President Nixon wishes he was a king instead of just a president. Then he wouldn't have to answer to anyone. Kings can get away with all kinds of stuff. It's too bad I wasn't running for king of Earth Club. But I wasn't, I was running for president, and so was Violet Dixon, and there you go.

"You'll never win, Penny Ellen Chambord," she said to me. "I am a seasoned political operative. I run a professional campaign."

Violet Dixon runs a dirty campaign. I made posters that said things like PENNY ELLEN FOR EARTH CLUB PRESIDENT and IF YOU'RE NOT PART OF THE SOLUTION, YOU'RE PART OF THE

POLLUTION. I happened, by total accident, to see Violet's posters before she could put them up. They said things like PENNY ELLEN CHAMBORD IS NO FRIEND OF THE EARTH and PENNY ELLEN—WOULD YOU TRUST HER WITH YOUR BABY? I mean, none of the seventh graders even have babies. But she put photographs of me on her posters, and in one of them I was dangling a baby upside down by its legs. In another, I was yelling at a dog.

And in the third one—well, in the third one I appeared to be smoking a cigarillo. I say "appeared to be" because although I did shout at that dog, and I did dangle that baby upside down, I definitely *did not, would not ever*, smoke a cigarillo. I spend too much time trying to wash that smell out of my hair from all of Mother's smoking.

On the third poster she wrote PENNY ELLEN CHAMBORD IS MORALLY BANKRUPT. I don't know exactly what that means, but if Violet Dixon wrote it about me, then it's not good.

I saw what she was trying to do. Violet Dixon, seasoned political operative, was trying to discredit me. She was trying to ruin my good name and make the whole seventh grade think I would make a lousy Earth Club president.

I figured out how she must have taken those photographs. I remember that day very well. In my own defense, that dog shouted at me first. I was minding my own business walking down Mathews Street, where Violet Dixon lives, when that dog ran after me and began to bark. I turned to yell, "Go home, ya dumb mutt!" but it wouldn't leave. It yipped around my ankles, and all I could do was keep walking.

That baby, which I recognized as the baby that belongs to Violet Dixon's neighbor, Mrs. Frisby, was crawling across the lawn toward me that same day as I was strolling through Violet Dixon's neighborhood. (I am not making it up when I say that Mrs. Frisby's baby looks a lot like a rat. It really does!) It was probably going after the dog.

"Don't let my baby crawl into the street!" cried Mrs. Frisby from her porch, where she was having a drink and a smoke. I reached for the baby, but it was as wobbly and hard to handle as one of Mother's molded gelatin salads. Instead of grabbing it under the arms, I grabbed it by the legs.

"Don't hold my baby by the legs!" cried Mrs. Frisby, putting down her drink and running across the lawn. She was still holding her cigarillo—I could tell it was a cigarillo because I recognized the smell from Mother.

Mrs. Frisby threw the burning cigarillo to the ground and took her rat-faced baby, and I reached down to pick up the cigarillo, since I did not want a fire to break out on Violet Dixon's street. I held it between my fingers the way Mother does and put my other hand on my hip and waited for Mrs. Frisby to calm down.

Well, Violet Dixon must be one heck of a photographer. She captured me holding that cigarillo, saying, "Mrs. Frisby, calm down," and my lips stuck out when I said "Frisby" just like I was blowing out smoke.

I asked Violet to hand over the photographs. She said she wouldn't. She said the people had a right to know. I said, "What people?" She ignored me.

Now Lulu's saying someone spied on Violet and broke into her house and tried to steal those photographs before she could put them all over the school. She's saying that someone was me. Best friends are supposed to be on your side, no matter what. That is what you sign up for when you promise to be someone's best friend. I don't think Lulu remembers that.

The whole thing has made such a stink that Miss Meacham won't be the Earth Club sponsor anymore, and Principal Cartland wants to ban all school clubs. He says they're a headache and cost too much money. But what is money when you are trying to save the earth?

Violet Dixon was being a creep. None of the photographs were real, but that doesn't matter to anyone. Even Lulu thinks I am not fit to run a school club. She thinks I'm not fit to be friends with, either.

I don't even want to say what I think of Lulu Van Allen.

Signed,

Penny Ellen Chambord

April 21, 1974

Today is my birthday. I am thirteen years old and president of nothing.

Last year on my birthday I went to the swimming pool with Lulu, and we had cake and ice cream afterward. This year I am celebrating in style, 100 percent by myself, although Mother will be there too.

"In style" means that I asked Mother to make a pineapple upside-down cake, and I've already eaten most of it in my room. Pineapple upside-down cake tastes better when you are alone, according to my research.

Lulu Van What's-Her-Name does not like pineapple. So I enjoyed my cake enormously even though Ruth wasn't there, and it's not easy to enjoy yourself when you miss your big sister.

In other news, this is the first day of Earth Week. A whole week for the earth is a very good idea. President Nixon just made a big deal about it, and I am glad to know that for once we agree on something. I wonder if he ever ran for president of his school's Earth Club. Would he have gotten himself into trouble over it, the way he has gotten into trouble over Watergate? I would not have voted for him. Still, I am going to tell Mother to stop throwing her cigarillos out the car window and to write letters about air pollution instead.

Signed,

Penny Ellen Chambord

April 22, 1974

Important update: Mother will not stop smoking cigarillos despite the fact that Ruth called all the way from college in Oberlin, Ohio, to tell her to quit. Ruth says smoking is bad not just for your body but for your soul. I have decided that I will only do things that are good for my soul. Like eating the rest of my pineapple upside-down cake.

Also, Mother will not stop throwing her cigarillos out the car window, so I have no choice but to take some direct action.

I have her cigarillos. And I will not give them back. I am running a campaign to make her stop smoking, whether she likes it or not.

That is very good for my soul.

Signed,

Penny Ellen Chambord

April 25, 1974

Mother has been very difficult lately.

"Where are my cigarillos?"

"What have you done with my cigarillos?"

"Every time I buy a pack of cigarillos, they disappear."

Et cetera.

I am running out of places to hide them.

I have also suggested that we buy more eggplant. Many nutritious meals can be made of eggplant, as Ruth wrote in her last letter, and it is very nearly the same as steak. Ruth says red meat is sending this country down the tubes, the way of the cigarillo. If Mother won't listen to me about the eggplant, I will have to find somewhere to hide the steak.

Update on the Van Allen front: Lulu has started a club. Without me. But with Violet Dixon. They're calling themselves the Roadside Clean-Up Crew. When I pointed out that the school did not have money for clubs anymore, they said they didn't need any money from the school, since they were just going to pick up trash, and trash is free.

Eggplants are kind of a purple color, kind of VIOLET. I'm going to chop one up right now, and I bet it will be DELICIOUS.

Signed,

Penny Ellen Chambord

April 26, 1974

Violet Dixon is a dope.

But enough about her.

She also looks like a fruit bat.

Some people think fruit bats are cute. I do not.

Why would someone who looks like a fruit bat and can't run an honest campaign for student office be a better best friend than someone who is as honest as the day is long? Answer: They would not.

If I am being honest, Violet does not look like a fruit bat. She looks like Scooby-Doo. And I am always honest.

For example, when I told Lulu that Violet Dixon is only two *N*'s away from Violent Nixon, I was only being honest. When I said that Nixon was a crook and a spy, and that Lulu should be very careful about associating with crooks, that was honest too.

Lulu does not appreciate honesty.

For another example, when I said that the only reason Violet Nixon-I-Mean-Dixon wanted to start a club with Lulu was because she had failed utterly to win an election against me, Lulu said I was just jealous.

That is *not* the truth. I am *not* jealous of Violet Dixon. As I said before, I am done writing about her. I would rather write about President Nixon.

I am not sure what I think of President Nixon. The newspaper says he broke all kinds of laws when he made some men do some spying for him in the Watergate Hotel. On the one hand, I do not approve of having people spy for you, but on the other hand, Earth Week has been a tremendous week for the earth.

I have many other things on my to-do list, now that I do not need to worry about running for student office. I am going to make sure that Mother does not get lung cancer from all that smoking. Also on my list are other things I can do to save the Earth. For example, I will not dump large barrels of toxic waste into the bay.

I am also going to find a *new best friend*. There must be a *hundred* people out there who would like to be best friends with someone like me.

Signed,

Penny Ellen Chambord

April 27, 1974

Well.

Well. If Lulu Van Allen wants to leave a bag full of cigarillo butts on my porch with the label "The thrill of victory, the agony of defeat!" on it, she's welcome to do it. Although she ought to be more original than to steal the motto of *The Wide World of Sports*. And since when does Lulu watch *The Wide World of Sports?* She is terrible at sports. Maybe Violet Dixon's bad influence is making her forget who she is.

The question is, did Lulu smoke all those cigarillos? Or did Violet Dixon?

The other question is, what will become of their souls?

Before this whole thing started, I was making a friendship bracelet for Lulu. A nice one, with her favorite colors, which are yellow and orange. We each have six friendship bracelets that we made for each other. The first time we made them, Lulu couldn't remember the word *bracelet*, so she called it a friendship tie. I liked that, because it tied us together.

I was working on number seven, but I don't know what I'll do with it now. Maybe I'll give it to my new best friend. Whoever that is.

Lulu Van Allen will simply <u>*never*</u> save the earth with Violet Dixon. It is not in their future. And if she thinks they're going to do it by picking up litter on the highway, let me tell her, there are more important things to do. What if the Cuyahoga River catches fire again? Why doesn't she go out to Ohio and clean that up? While she's out there, she could say hello to Ruth and tell her that her sister misses her.

I was so mad, I was going to walk right over to Lulu's and pour those cigarillo butts out on her mother's rock garden. Let Lulu try to clean <u>*that*</u> up!

But in the end I remembered that I am a friend of the earth, never mind what Violet Dixon says about me, and friends of the earth don't do things like that.

Signed,

Penny Ellen Chambord

Cora

After

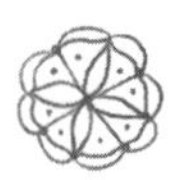

That was it. Well, almost it. After the last entry, Penny Ellen had left a few blank pages, as if her feelings, like Cora's, were too big and tangled up to fit in a diary.

Too big, Cora thought, even for the biggest curbside bins, too big for the city trucks that hauled everything away.

Then, on the fourth page, Penny Ellen had written in very small letters: *Oh, Lulu.*

"Oh, Lulu," Cora murmured, and then, with a jolt of self-pity, she whispered, "Oh, Cora. Oh, Sybella."

What had happened to Penny Ellen and Lulu's friendship? Did they make up? Cora was still thinking about it when Kyle found her in the locker room, saying that they were ready to leave.

As they walked home, Cora wondered if the Mathews Street in the diary was the Mathews Street in Berkeley, where the Fish House was. Dr. Davis had taken them on a bike tour of "green" buildings in Berkeley over the summer, and now Cora knew all about the Fish House. It was round, and it looked like a cross between a spaceship and a sea creature. It was supposed to be earthquake-proof. Indestructible.

If Penny Ellen had walked down Mathews Street, then maybe she'd walked down Cora's street sometime too. Maybe Penny Ellen and all her feelings had been right there in Berkeley, which made Cora feel better somehow, knowing that lots of people had friend problems, like Dani said, even if Penny Ellen's problems had been a long time ago. Maybe Penny Ellen had also gone to Cora's school and shopped at the Berkeley Bowl with her dad.

She never mentioned a dad in the diary, though. And then Cora remembered that the indestructible Fish House wasn't built yet in 1974, and her school was newer than that too. Even the Berkeley Bowl might not have been there in 1974. Penny Ellen would have walked around a totally different Berkeley, and all the comfort Cora had started to feel fell away like leaves off a tree.

When she got home, Cora crawled under her blanket with her half of Penny Ellen's diary to read it again, but it didn't give her any better answers than the first time. She desperately wanted to know the end of the story, to know if everything had turned out well for Penny Ellen and Lulu, but for that, she'd need the other half of the diary.

And Sybella had that.

Was Sybella reading it? Was she wondering the same things about friends and different lives and indestructible places? Or maybe she'd tried to recycle it after all, even though it was supposed to be thrown away.

"Cora?"

Underneath her wool blanket, Cora was running out of air. She poked her head out, reluctantly, and bumped into Kyle, who was about to poke his head under the blanket. "Ow!"

"Sorry," said Kyle, rubbing his forehead. "I just came to see if you were okay."

"I'm fine," said Cora.

She was not fine. How could she be? She replayed Marnie's words from earlier: "Sybella Seward is on my team." Was that how it was going to be from now on—Sybella and Marnie were a team, and Cora was just an alternate? Was she now the last person anyone wanted, the one on the sidelines who was only useful if it was absolutely the last choice?

The truth was, she didn't even feel like an alternate. She had no position. She wasn't part of the game at all anymore.

She imagined Sybella calling Marnie Stoll, the Friend-Stealing Troll, at that very minute to invite her over for some activity that had nothing to do with trash. Maybe they were still wearing their matching gloves.

Kyle sat on the edge of her bed. "That was fun today. The Trashlympics. Wasn't it?"

Cora grunted.

"You know what I loved most about it?" said Kyle. As if there were many things to love about spending the day with garbage. "Most of all, I felt like I had some control. Like, if there's a problem, maybe I can do something to fix it. You know that time-lapse video of the landfill?"

Cora knew the video. She had seen it dozens of times. It was called "Hopeless Waste," and it showed trash piling up at the transfer station as people dropped off bags and boxes. In the background, the skies went from early-morning pink to blue and then sunny and then dark and back again, and all the time trash just piled and piled. It was a project from one of Dr. Davis's former research students, and kids watched it in classrooms all over the country.

Classrooms, Cora thought, where kids probably saw it and promised to do better and then did exactly the same thing they'd always done: They threw everything away.

"When I watched that, I felt terrible," Kyle continued. "But when I did the Trashlympics, I felt powerful."

Only Kyle would feel powerful playing with trash. Although, after reading the diary, Cora knew what he meant. It did feel good to be doing something that she knew was right.

Like Penny Ellen, who had been determined to do what she thought was right. She'd wanted to save the earth and her mother's lungs. Cora wondered too about the rest of her life. What happened to someone whose feelings were too big to fit on paper?

Sybella

After

Sybella had begged her parents to take her to McGinnis's on her birthday—on the official Aquafabian birthday—because she'd hoped Cora and Kyle would be there. Maybe if she saw them outside of school, if they were somewhere that only had happy memories, all the bad would just slip away.

The plan had failed. Like bad magic, Cora had ended up with fries in her hair, and Sybella had been too nervous to talk to her. The friendship bracelet fiasco had only made it worse. It was supposed to be a signal to Cora that Sybella wanted to be friends again. She hadn't realized until it was too late that the bracelet was one of the ones she'd cut off hurriedly after that sad weekend in Sausalito, because it was too mashed and knotted to untie.

What kind of signal was that?

As soon as she got home from her birthday dinner, she put away the Stellar Suzy Glam n' Jam Home Nail Salon she'd gotten from her parents and lay down on her bed. She picked up the stress ball she always left on her pillow. It was blue and green and looked vaguely like Earth, although none of the continents or landmasses looked right. Greenland was attached to the Arctic, and there was an extra chunk of land between North America and Asia. She used to think that was Aquafaba, risen out of the water like Atlantis, but now she squeezed it, smashing the mystery land back into the ocean, and felt a little better.

She didn't hate Aquafaba, though, or Cora or Kyle or any of the games they had played. She was just . . . sad. She tried to think of a better word—her mother was always teaching her new words to improve her vocabulary—but nothing came. Just *sad*.

She knew from watching her parents argue and make up that usually both people had to say "sorry" after a fight. Both sides had to try to make things right, and they had to really mean it. But her parents' arguments never lasted longer than a day. She and Cora had been fighting for weeks.

She had avoided most of the Trash Team meetings, choosing Chess Club in the library instead. She'd tried talking to Cora, but that hadn't worked. It was easier to avoid her. She ended up avoiding Kyle a lot too, even though she didn't think he was mad at her. He was stuck in the middle, and that wasn't fair, either.

When she came up with the birthday plan a week ago, in a flurry of hope, she'd thought that everything might be fixed by now. Why was friendship, which had been so simple ever since second grade, suddenly so hard?

Her mother opened her bedroom door. "Sy? Aren't you supposed to be working on your art project?"

The Upcycle Your Trash art contest was next Saturday, a week away. She'd had an idea for a project, but now it didn't seem right. The materials were laid out in a corner of her room, waiting.

"I am working on it?" she said, like a question, and her mother shook her head.

"Put the time in now," she said. "You never regret putting time in where it really matters."

Sybella crawled off her bed and over to her project. "It's so hard, Mom." She was only partly talking about the art project.

"I know," said her mom, and Sybella wondered if they were talking about the same thing.

"Look, Sy, I know you and Cora are having a hard time, but that won't last. Every road has bumps. You're just in the bumpy spot. You'll move past it."

"Maybe," said Sybella. But she wasn't sure. She surveyed her road, and all she saw were bumps, potholes, and roadkill. But she hugged her mom, because she was only trying to help, and promised to work on her art project.

She wasn't feeling any better at breakfast the next morning, though. "Do I have to go to the Trashlympics today?" she asked over her buttermilk pancakes.

"Did you sign up to go to the Trashlympics today?" asked her mom.

"Yes," she said, although her mom already knew the answer. Sybella and her parents had been collecting their trash all week in preparation for the Trash-In.

"Then you're going to the Trashlympics today, Sy. Did you find the gloves I left on your desk?"

The gloves were shiny red, and her mom had sewn artificial daisies around the cuffs and yellow bows on the back of each hand. They were what a princess might wear to sort her trash. Sybella might have liked them when she was five years old and she loved to stand out, but not when she was eleven and she wanted to disappear.

After breakfast, Sybella changed into an old pair of jeans and a shirt with an astronaut cat on it and asked her dad if they had any other rubber gloves.

"What about the ones your mom gave you?"

"They're kind of too nice for touching a bunch of

garbage." *And kind of silly,* she thought, but she kept that to herself.

"You're going to be dealing with top-of-the-line Seward family *gar-bahge,*" said her dad, tying up a black trash bag and handing it to Sybella. "I think your gloves are perfect."

Sybella knew when she was defeated. She stuffed the gloves into her pocket and heaved the garbage bag out to the car. *Don't bring really gross stuff!!* the flyer said, so she'd left all the food scraps in the compost bucket and let her old gum stay stuck to the bottom of the garbage can in her room.

Her mom came out to get a goodbye hug, then she put her hands on Sybella's shoulders and looked her over. "Are you okay, Sy? You don't look like your usual self."

Sybella leaned into her mom. "I'm nervous, I guess."

She didn't say what she was nervous about, but her mom didn't have to be told. "Maybe today's the day you smooth out some of those bumps, then."

"What if I can't?"

"You'll still be my amazing daughter, and you have time to figure the rest of it out."

"You think I can?" asked Sybella.

Her mother squeezed her shoulders. "You *and* Cora.

One person can't fix a problem that two people made."

Sybella wasn't sure if that made her feel better, because she didn't have to fix things by herself, or worse, because she *couldn't* fix things by herself.

"So, Trashlympics," said her dad as they drove to the campus field house where Sybella and her garbage were going to spend the day. "If you win, do you bring home the gold or the . . . *mold*?" He grinned and waited for Sybella's reaction.

"Blech," she said, leaning against the window. And she meant it. Blech to dad jokes and Trashlympics and all trash activities, and blech to the whole dumb situation. At the beginning of the year, she'd pictured being on a Trashlympics team with Cora and Kyle, wearing the friendship bracelets they'd made. Now—just *blech*.

Her dad pulled into the parking lot and, reluctantly, she got out and yanked her trash bag out of the car. She pulled so hard, one of the drawstring handles snapped and her bag gaped open.

"Could this get any worse?" she muttered. That question might have been a magic spell, because instantly everything got worse. A metallic purple Jeep parked next to her car, and Marnie Stoll stared at her from the backseat.

"Syyyyybellllllllaaaaaa!" Marnie cried, but Sybella

didn't wait around to find out what Marnie wanted.

She headed for the field house ahead of her dad, trying to outrun Marnie, but her trash bag weighed her down, and she limped along with it bumping against her leg. Marnie, unsurprisingly trash-free, caught up and even skipped ahead in her striped leg warmers, saying, "I'm so happy we're a team finally!"

Sybella didn't want to talk to her at all, but she was so irritated at Marnie, who thought she could have everything just because she wanted it, that before she could stop herself, she blurted, "We're not. You don't even care about the environment. You throw your soda cans in the trash every lunchtime."

Marnie almost looked hurt. "It's so the Trash Team can learn how to separate trash from recyclables."

That sounded reasonable, but Sybella didn't believe Marnie. "You put your oranges in plastic bags! When they still have their skin on! And you throw the bags away! You don't even reuse them."

Marnie blinked. She looked toward the gym. "Hey, look, it's your former best friend." Marnie skipped toward the door. Sybella glimpsed Cora trying to hang something on the door, but then Cora dropped her poster and disappeared into the gym.

When Sybella got to the gym, she couldn't see Cora in any of the small groups of kids and grown-ups who filled the basketball court. Kyle was helping his dad register people and showing them where to go for all the different events. Juniper was marking lanes for the relay race with masking tape. Bags of trash were everywhere.

She didn't see Cora until she looked up to the top of the bleachers, where Cora leaned against the wall with her chin in her hands.

Sybella wondered if her mother had been right after all. Was it really a problem that two people had made? Or had Cora made the problem, and should Cora be the one to fix it? Sybella had tried reaching out. Maybe now it was Cora's turn to reach out instead of running away.

Sybella had no team anymore, so she had decided to do the sorting and a couple of individual events and then sit out the team events, hoping her dad wouldn't mind.

"Let's get you registered, sweetheart," said her dad, pointing to the table.

Going to the registration table meant getting close to Marnie again, and Sybella hesitated. "Can you do it for me? I have to, um, sort through my bag."

"Isn't that what you do *after* you register?"

"I have to pre-sort it," she said desperately. "To get ready for the event. Can you sign me in?" She knew the look on her dad's face. He was going to make her go over to the registration table, because she was old enough to start doing things for herself.

Before he could start talking about how sometimes you had to take the bull by the horns, sit in the driver's seat, and chart your own course (he was always saying things like that), Sybella pulled the red gloves out of her back pocket. She slipped them on and held them up, wiggling her fingers. "Please?"

"Your mom did a great job with those gloves," he said. Sybella knew she'd won.

Sybella's dad went to the registration table, where Marnie was waving her arms and saying something loud about teams. Then she pointed straight at Sybella like she was putting a curse on her. Cora's head snapped up. She stared at Sybella from across the gym, and a jolt went through Sybella's whole body.

It was a curse. As her dad explained when he returned, Marnie wanted to do the trash relay, but you couldn't do the trash relay unless you had at least one teammate. So Marnie had claimed Sybella, and her dad, as Sybella's official representative, had agreed.

"More trash points!" he said, heading for the bleachers. "How great is that?"

Marnie skipped over to Sybella. "I am so going to win this thing," she said, pulling up her leg warmers and cracking her knuckles. "I mean, we. Because we're a team, right? Team Mar-bella! I'll be captain."

This wasn't just a bump in the road. It felt like an earthquake. *Mar-bella?* No. There was no name for their team—they weren't even a real team!

She knew she couldn't avoid Marnie all day, but instead of answering her, Sybella hauled her bag to the corner of the gym, where the Trash-In was happening. She knew how to sort almost every item, even ones that weren't hers. After spending so much time with Cora and Kyle, she hardly had to think about it.

Sybella's hands were getting sweaty inside her rubber gloves, so she took them off before the Trash and Dash, setting them on one of the bleachers, and tried to dry her hands on her jeans. Marnie swooped in and grabbed a glove. "I'll wear one and you wear one," she said, stretching a glove over her right hand.

Marnie held out her red glove for a fist bump. Sybella wanted to leave her hanging there, but she hated to look like a bad sport in front of everyone. She bumped Marnie's glove with her own, but she couldn't bring herself to smile.

The last event, Capture the Trash, took the whole court. Anyone who wasn't playing sat on the bleachers to watch, including Cora. Sybella had tried all day to forget that Cora was there, and because she discovered she was actually having fun, despite the Marnie-ness of Marnie, it had worked. Until now.

"Too bad you don't have matching team shirts for us," said Marnie.

Because they weren't a real team! Despite what Marnie thought, they had never been a real team. She was trying to work out how to grab her glove back when Dani came up and told them they needed one more person on their team to play Capture the Trash.

Sybella purposely didn't look Cora's way again. If Cora wanted to be on Sybella's team, she could ask. But she would never ask.

So Marnie found Maddie, a girl Sybella knew a little from school. Maddie didn't look like she wanted to be there, but Marnie was hard to say no to, especially when she had you by the wrist and was dragging you across the basketball court.

The whistle blew, and Sybella started running. She was not the fastest runner in their class, but she was agile and she loved to move. She dodged the other players easily, and after a couple of trips across the court, she thought she might actually win. But Marnie Marnie-d the whole thing up by arguing with Maddie and running onto the court, earning herself a penalty, and Maddie wound up with a sprained ankle.

Then Dani told Cora to join their team. Sybella

breathed deeply and kept on playing. It should have been great to be on the same team. That's how they had planned it months ago, but now it was awkward. Cora was slower than usual, and Sybella began to wonder if she was doing it on purpose. But then suddenly Cora sped up and made a wild grab for the same thing Sybella was going for, a red book, and they ended up sprawled on the floor, each holding half, until Cora scrambled to her feet and ran away, moving faster than she had during the entire game.

Sybella tossed the torn book to the floor, along with her single red glove. Dr. Davis was making an announcement about the winners of each event, and how many trash points everyone had, but Sybella didn't want to listen. "Let's go," she said to her dad.

"What about your gloves?"

Marnie had disappeared after the whistle blew, taking one of Sybella's gloves with her. Maybe she didn't want to hear the final count, either, because she knew she hadn't won this thing after all.

Sybella reached for the left glove. The book, next to it on the floor, was open to a drawing of an owl in a Robin Hood hat and the words *Give a Hoot! Don't Pollute* in cramped block lettering above it.

It wasn't a great drawing, but Sybella recognized that it must have taken someone a lot of time. She picked the book up and saw the words written in messy handwriting underneath the owl: *I don't give a hoot about anything.*

Sybella felt sorry for whoever had drawn the owl. Did they really not give a hoot about anything, or were they just angry? Cora said that sometimes: *I don't care. I hate everything.* Kyle was the opposite. He cared about everything and loved everyone. But, Sybella reminded herself, she wasn't thinking about them.

The book was obviously someone's diary or notebook, so how had it ended up in a pile of trash at the Trashlympics? Maybe she could find out who it belonged to. She looked for Dani, but she was busy. She decided to take it home and bring it to school on Friday, when the Trash Team was scheduled to meet for the last time.

She picked up the half-diary, along with her single glove, and took them both home, wondering if either one would get back together with its other half.

She told herself she wouldn't read the diary, since it was obviously someone's property, but then she realized it might give her some clues about who it belonged to, like opening a lost wallet to look for a driver's license.

On the page after the owl, she saw a date: May 1, 1974. A long time ago, more than forty years. So whoever wrote it could be in their fifties, or maybe even older. Old enough that probably they didn't care about a diary from when they were a kid. Reading something that old wasn't snooping, it was historical research. Maybe she could even use it for a history project one day.

Pieces for her art project were still spread across the floor, but Sybella ignored them and lay on her bed to read.

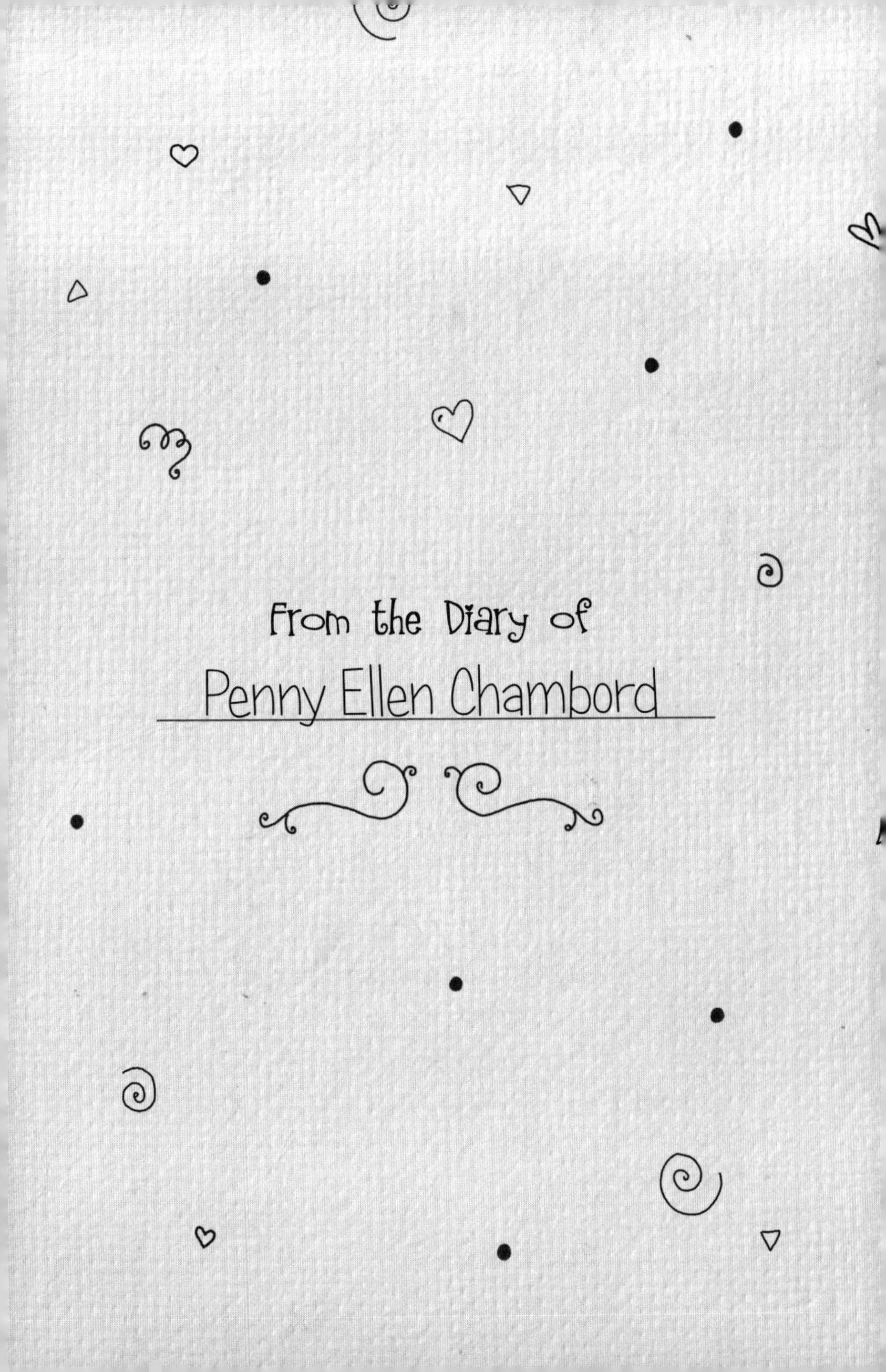
From the Diary of
Penny Ellen Chambord

~~April 31, 1974~~ May 1, 1974

May 1 is also known as May Day, and "mayday" is what you say when you need help.

I need help.

I've made a real mess, and I don't know how I'm going to clean everything up.

I saw Lulu and Violet Dixon Who Looks Like President Nixon picking up trash in the park. I hugged the side fence so as not to get too close to them, but they saw me anyway. Violet strode right up to me and dropped a worm on my right shoe. Mother just bought me those shoes from Sears too. The worm didn't hurt it any, and I put the worm in a nice flowerbed so it could resume its life.

Violet marched off, and I stuck out my tongue at her as she went.

Lulu hung back. She wouldn't even look at me. She wouldn't look at Violet, either, but that didn't make me feel any better. She just went on picking up trash and putting it in a bag, and I was too nervous and worm-trail-covered to go up to her and say, "I'm sorry."

So I will say it here, and if Lulu ever breaks into my house and reads my diary (and she might), then she will read my apology.

Here goes nothing:

1. Lulu Van Allen, I am sorry I broke into your house and read your diary.

2. Lulu Van Allen, I am sorry I stole your diary and pretended I had no earthly idea what you were talking about when you asked me to give it back.

3. Lulu Van Allen, I am sorry I left a cigarillo butt in an ashtray on your dresser so you would know I had been there—I did not smoke the cigarillo, it was one of Mother's, along with the ashtray, which I found in the shower—and I am sorry that I also lied about that.

4. Lulu Van Allen, I am mostly very, very sorry about everything that happened leading up to the time when I broke into your house, read your diary, stole your diary, and left a trail of cigarillo butts for you to find me. I have a terrible thirst for revenge and . . .

5. I am very sorry about that too.

Yesterday I saw on the news that President Nixon handed over transcripts of the Watergate tapes to Congress. The transcript is the written record of all the things that he said on those tapes, and I think he's in even more hot water now.

I am in hot water myself. I am a lot nicer than President Nixon, but I too have to fess up to all my crimes.

So here it is.

I, the undersigned, Penny Ellen Chambord, do solemnly swear that I ruined Violet Dixon's life. At least, I tried to. Here is the transcript of how it happened.

Wednesday, April 17, 1974, 3:04 p.m.

Lulu Van Allen (LVA): I'm so bored. We should do something fun.

Penny Ellen Chambord (PEC): You wanna play Double Dutch?

LVA: You can't play Double Dutch with only two people.

PEC: You wanna get chocolate-covered frozen bananas from Baskin-Robbins?

LVA: Yeah, okay.

3:30 p.m.

PEC: How could they be out of chocolate-covered frozen bananas? Chocolate-covered bananas are the most important treat known to mankind.

(It doesn't show on the transcript that PEC is sulking, but she is.)

LVA: I don't know. What do you want to do now?

(It doesn't show on the transcript that LVA is eating a single scoop of pink bubble gum ice cream, but she is.)

PEC: Let's go spy on Violet Dixon.

End transcript.

Maybe I didn't go so far as to say, "Let's go spy on Violet Dixon." Maybe I just said, "Let's go see what Violet Dixon is up to." And Lulu gave me a funny look, because she knew that Violet Dixon was running for president of Earth Club and that I was also running for president of Earth Club, and that I had said something to Violet Dixon the day before that wasn't very professional.

What I said was, "I'm going to ruin your life, Violet Dixon."

I should not have said it. But politics is a high-stakes game, and I was feeling kind of put out that anyone else was going to run for president of _my_ club. I don't think Violet Dixon likes the earth all that much. I just think she doesn't like me.

Lulu gave me that funny look, but she came with me to "see" Violet Dixon all the same. From my position in one of Mrs. Dixon's flowerbeds, I could see that Violet was in her room, sitting on her bed and pretending to do her homework like she always did after school. How did I know that? This was not the first time I had gone to see what Violet Dixon was up to.

There is a thing that people who are running for office do to try to win. It's called "discrediting the other candidate." I saw it on the news. They try to dig up some dirt on their opponent and tell everyone about it, so that everyone will vote for them instead of for their opponent. I needed some dirt on Violet Dixon, but Violet wasn't cooperating. Homework doesn't count as dirt.

"Look what she's doing," I told Lulu. "Come here and see."

Lulu looked nervous, but she came into the flowerbed and peeked into Violet's window. "She's doing her homework."

"She wants you to *think* she's doing her homework," I said. "Do you know what she's really doing? She's plotting. Against me. I can tell by the way she's gripping her pencil."

"No, she's doing long division," said Lulu. "I can tell by the way she's got her long division homework sheet in her lap."

"Violet Dixon is a real sneak," I said. "That's not long division. That's all code. Just give me a minute, and I'll decode it and tell you what it says."

Lulu would not give me a minute. She said, "Penny Ellen, we are best friends and everything, but I do not approve of spying on people. I am going home."

"What are you going to do at home?" I asked.

"I am going to write in my diary," said Lulu.

"I hope your diary takes a flying leap," I said.

I would not normally say that to Lulu, but politics does funny things to people.

Lulu frowned at me and left.

At the time, I was not sorry to see her go. But after about five minutes, something happened that I was very sorry Lulu was not there to see.

Violet finished up her long division code writing and brushed her hair. She left her room and came back with a bag of Granny Goose potato chips and a Dr. Pepper. She put them down on her desk, and then she looked over her shoulder. This is an important detail because it shows that she was worried about being found out.

Well, she should have been worried. Because what I saw next was astonishing.

She reached under her mattress and removed a key. With the key, she opened the kneehole drawer of her desk. And out of that drawer, she took three 8-x-10 black-and-white photographs and spread them on her desk, like she was bringing evidence before a judge. I had to strain to see them without being discovered, but I managed to do it because I am dedicated to my work.

That was how I found out that Violet was running a dirty campaign. At the time I did not know how she got those photographs of me with the dog and the baby and the cigarillo, but I knew she was up to no good. I knew she was going to use them against me.

I had to tell Lulu. And I had to get proof.

The only proof I could think of was the photographs themselves. But they were inside Violet's house. Which meant that _I_ had to get inside Violet's house.

I knew from my careful observations that Violet went to swimming lessons on Wednesdays at 4:30 p.m. She always packed up her swimsuit and her goggles, which is how I knew she went to swimming lessons.

I didn't have to wait long. Violet packed up her swimsuit and goggles and left her room. The photographs were sitting on her desk. After only a minute, however, she came back, opened the kneehole drawer, put the photographs in, and locked it. She put the key back under her mattress, because she is a fool.

Everyone knows thieves look under your mattress first. Even if I hadn't already known that Violet kept her key under her mattress, I would have looked there first.

Violet left her room, and I scrambled to a better hiding place, because I knew she was going to appear at her side door and walk to the pool. She did so, calling,

"Bye, Mom!" as she left. It was then that I made my move.

In hindsight (which means "looking back"), it was a terrible move. But I made it all the same. I creeped over to her side door and opened it. I went in. I knew where her room was, so I headed in that direction, keeping low to the ground.

Then I heard it.

Bark!

It was that dog.

It was the very same dumb mutt I had shouted at in that photograph, and it was coming at me down Violet Dixon's hallway.

Now, when someone calls out "Bye, Mom!" as they leave to go somewhere, you should figure that somewhere close by, there is a mom. I heard Violet say that, but I didn't put two and two together. Not only did the dog come running at me, bark-bark-barking, and grab one of my shoelaces in its teeth as I lay on the ground, squirming, but a tall woman in a housedress came into the hallway from somewhere and said, "I'm very sorry, dear, but Violet is at her swimming lesson."

I stood up, brushed myself off, and said with great dignity, "Sorry to disturb you, ma'am."

I think she might have let me go with that if I hadn't lost my temper at her dog and shouted, "Why don't you take a flying leap, ya dumb mutt!"

"How dare you speak to Lancelot that way!" said Mrs. Dixon. "I don't know where Violet picks up her friends these days, but I won't have rudeness toward dogs in this house."

Mother was called in, and I was still there explaining myself when Violet returned from her swimming lesson. She took one look at me and said, "I'll get you for this, Penny Ellen Chambord."

And Lulu wasn't there to see the unfairness of it all.

The next day at school, Lulu wouldn't sit with me before the first bell rang, and she wouldn't play tetherball with me. She hardly even looked at me, except to tell me how disappointed she was in me. That was because Violet Dixon was always in the way. Violet ratted me out to Lulu, and then she clung to Lulu like Saran Wrap.

We happened to be washing our hands together in

the girls' restroom at the same time, and I said, "Lulu, I have to tell you something."

Lulu wouldn't listen. She asked me, "Did you break into Violet's house yesterday?"

"No," I said. Walking through an unlocked door is *not* breaking in.

"Violet says you stole some photographs she was going to use on her campaign posters," she said.

"I didn't!" I said. "She's lying! I couldn't even get into her room because her dumb dog bit me while I was crawling down her hallway!"

And then I realized I was beat. I had given myself up, and Lulu looked even more disappointed.

I tried to explain to her how Violet had taken those photos and how she was the bad guy in all this, not me, but Lulu just said, "How do I know you're not lying, Penny Ellen?"

"Because I'm not!" I said. But that's not very good proof, and even though she's supposed to be my best friend, I don't think Lulu believed me.

For the rest of the day, Lulu and Violet walked around

with their heads practically stuck together. They were always whispering. I figured they were whispering about me. I tried to hear what they were saying, but every time I got close enough, they moved away.

I did hear one thing. I heard Lulu say, "I wrote it all down in my diary." And I just knew that whatever it was, it was about me. She was going to show it to Violet, and they were going to discredit me some more.

I had lost a friend, but I wasn't going to lose the election, which was supposed to happen on Friday. I know now that they weren't talking about me at all. They were talking about the Roadside Clean-Up Crew, this new club they were going to start without me. But I didn't know it then, which is why I decided to do what I did next.

Breaking into Lulu Van Allen's house was a lot easier than breaking into Violet Dixon's. For one thing, no spying was necessary. I knew where everything was, and I knew when Lulu would be visiting her grandmother and learning to darn socks. For another, I could just walk right in like I did all the time and say to Lulu's mother that I had forgotten something in Lulu's room. Which I had. I had forgotten to leave my friendship bracelets right on her desk, so she would know that as far as I was concerned, we weren't friends anymore, so there.

I wanted to read her diary too, because I needed to find out what she was thinking. I needed to find out if any of her thinking was about me.

I took her big scissors and snipped those bracelets off my wrist. Some of them I chopped right in half. I left the pile of them on her desk with a note that said, *You can keep your friendship ties to yourself.* Then I went for her diary, because of course I knew she kept it right under her mattress. Best friends (former best friends) know these things about each other. But what have I said about people who keep things under their mattresses?

I did find it. I did steal it. I left Mother's second-favorite ashtray, the one shaped like my hand and painted pink, on Lulu's desk, full of cigarillo butts, because I wanted Lulu's mother to think she had taken up smoking. And then I jumped out of Lulu's window.

Lulu lives on the first floor, like Violet Dixon. She has pretty flowers under her window, like Violet Dixon. I crushed those flowers under my Sears loafers, just like I crushed Violet Dixon's, and took off down the street. I scattered some of those cigarillo butts as I went, because Lulu can't stand to see a mess on the ground. She would pick them up, following the trail. And I hoped, even after all our problems, that Lulu Van Allen would want to find me.

The next day, the Earth Club election was canceled because there was no money left in the school budget to save the earth. So nobody won.

What I want to say, Lulu, if you're reading this, and I don't see why you wouldn't be, what I want to say is that I wish we had all won. I do not mean I wish we had all won the election. That would be impossible. I mean that we lost—completely. I lost you, and you lost me, and even mean old Violet Dixon probably lost something too, and I'm sorry about that. I'm sorrier than all the pink bubble gum ice cream and chocolate-covered frozen bananas in the world.

Cora

Now

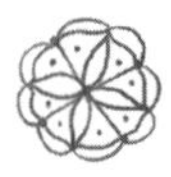

Cora stared at the horizon through the windows of the classroom on the *Alleen B.* She tried memorizing the fish posters, because she knew Dr. Davis would ask her what she had learned and she wanted to be able to say she had learned something, but she gave up after three fish.

Sybella was still measuring fish. Most of the fish seemed very ordinary. Where were the colorful fish? Or the giant sharks? Or the mermaids?

She imagined Sybella, right now, pulling a tiny mer-girl out of the net, plopping her into the right tank, and pulling her out later to measure from the tip of her nose to her caudal peduncle, which was how you measured a fish, according to the posters.

Cora imagined that she was the mer-girl, that an

enormous Sybella, with her Berry Berry Burgundy nails, pulled her from the tank by the tail and tried to get her to lie flat on the measuring board.

"Not this one," Sybella might say. "This one isn't even worth measuring. It's just trash."

Jilly poked her head into the classroom again. "Lunch," she said, pointing over her shoulder. They weren't going to let Cora eat her lunch indoors.

"Okay," said Cora. "I'll come out. I'm just finishing something."

Jilly looked puzzled. "Finishing what?"

"Just measuring something," said Cora, although she knew she looked like she was doing nothing at all.

"Gotcha," said Jilly, in the same way you might say, "Uh-huh, sure you are." "I'll save you a sandwich." She left, and Cora kept measuring.

Obviously she wasn't measuring fish, or any other thing you could grab from a touch tank and lay down on a mat. She was, very quickly and very clumsily, taking measure of herself. Not her height or her weight, because she wasn't concerned about those, but the measure of her whole self. Of herself as a person and a friend.

If Sybella pulled Cora out of the tank and held her by the tail, if Sybella said she was not worth measuring, it would be because Cora was not a good enough friend.

Watching Sybella working alongside Jilly and Jen,

sorting fish and laughing, Cora realized something: Sybella was an optimist, like Kyle. She might be first at everything, but that was only because she was trying to make everything the best it could be, so she tried as hard as she could. Aquafaba was better with her in it.

At the very least, Cora should have been honest with Sybella, but she hadn't even been able to do that. She'd been a terrible friend. She would have thrown herself back, if she had pulled herself out of the ocean.

Not worth measuring.

Cora looked out at the sorting tanks. The others weren't waiting for her. The two instructors were eating their sandwiches and laughing about something, and Sybella, who was first at everything and had probably already finished her sandwich, was letting her fingers drag in the water of one of the tanks. Then she stood up and put her whole hand in a tank.

Of course she's getting right back to work, Cora thought.

Sybella grabbed a fish, just bigger than her two hands clasped together, and looked it in the eye. She glanced at the instructors, who weren't paying any attention to her. Jilly was showing the other instructor something on her phone. Then, as Cora watched, Sybella whispered something to the fish and tossed it over the side of the *Alleen B.*

It must have been a mistake. They had just trawled

for all these fish. They were supposed to measure them first, then toss them back. Sybella liked to do things the right way. She was a good listener. A team player. She wouldn't deliberately mess up the project.

Cora watched her quickly grab another fish, whisper to it, and toss it, and by the time she'd picked up the third fish, the other instructor was saying, "Hey, quit that! We haven't measured those yet!"

But Sybella was not a quitter. She threw the fish that was in her hands and went for one of the five-gallon buckets, where fish waited before being sorted. She tried to drag it to the side and lift it, but five gallons of water plus fish is very heavy, and Sybella was struggling to get it off the deck. She squatted down, put her arms around the bucket, and tried to stand. Cora saw one of Sybella's feet slide out from under her, even on the no-slip rubber mat, and the bucket tipped, spilling fish and fish water in a wave across the deck.

Sybella looked directly at Cora as she called out, in the voice that had once carried so clearly across the playground, *"Aquafaba patria est!"*

"What are you doing?" shouted Jilly, and by now both instructors were on their feet, trying to pull Sybella up, catch fish, and sluice the water back into the bay.

"What are you doing?" must have been a rhetorical question, because Jilly didn't say anything else after

Sybella made her declaration. She just scrambled around, trying to pick up fish, while Jen brought Sybella into the classroom and sat her down firmly next to Cora.

"Stay here while I talk to the skipper, both of you," she said. "I'm going to have to tell her to head back to the dock early. You kids. I swear. Who throws fish back before they've been measured?"

"I saw them jump," said Cora quickly. "She was trying to measure them, but they jumped. She didn't throw them. It was all just a horrible mistake." That was a lie, but Cora didn't mind lying for a good reason.

Jen frowned and left the girls together.

For a moment the girls said nothing. Cora looked one way, and Sybella looked the other. Then, very quietly, Cora repeated Sybella's words, this time as a question.

"Aquafaba patria est?"

Sybella

What Happened

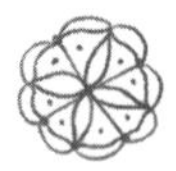

On her first day of second grade at Thurgood Marshall Elementary, Sybella was prepared to explore the polar wastes alone. She put on her winter coat and cinched the hood around her face, even though her mother told her it would mess up her hair.

Within a couple of weeks, she had found two friends, learned a handful of secret words, and discovered one imaginary kingdom with a very weird name.

As twins, Cora and Kyle were close and full of shared experiences. Sybella wondered what it was like to be that close to someone, even—or maybe especially—to someone who was so different from you.

Kyle was always smiling, and Cora didn't smile a lot, but her eyes lit up when she was happy about something.

Kyle was outgoing, and Cora kept to herself, but that just made everything she said to Sybella more interesting.

Three was a crowd, some people said, or three was the most awkward number for a group, since someone was always bound to get left out. But Sybella knew, thanks to her chemical engineer parents, that three was also a very stable arrangement, triangular, the most favored shape in nature. And none of the Aquafabians ever felt left out.

There was always something new happening in Aquafaba. Kyle wanted to fill their kingdom with dogs. Imaginary ones, because he wasn't allowed to have a real one. "Dogs make everything better!" he explained.

Cora wanted waffles to be their official food, which was fine with Sybella. "Waffles make everything double better," Cora had added.

Sybella tried showing Cora how to climb to the top of the playground bars, but Cora didn't want to, and that was all right. Sybella brought slices of pepperoni to share with the twins, since it was something they never got to eat at home, and they shared Cora's chocolate milk at lunchtime, drinking it through straws made of long, hollow pasta. That was weird at first, but the better she got to know Cora and Kyle, the less weird it seemed.

"It's compostable," Cora said when Sybella had asked why. That was the answer to many of the questions she asked Cora about the things she did, like wrapping her sandwiches in waxed paper.

Through third and fourth grade they grew into even better friends. It didn't matter that they hadn't "extended themselves" and made new friends, the way their teachers were always telling them to do. Why should they extend themselves when they were already the perfect shape?

And then there was fifth grade. Fifth grade was going to be the very best year. The three mer-friends were at the top of the school and at the top of their game. Sybella noticed a shift in the way they played the Aquafaba game by fifth grade, like it wasn't so much a game as a way of being. Like being in your family or your neighborhood. You didn't have to think about it—you just *were.*

More and more of their game seeped into reality, like a persistent water drip. Water could carve through stone, given enough time. They learned that from a geology documentary. And they saw it happening here and there: little tracks left in the real world by their imaginations.

One Friday in March, they were crouching on the platform at the top of the slide at afternoon recess, talking about the art contest. Cora had left her jacket inside, and she was wearing Sybella's scarf around her shoulders.

"What are you making for the contest?" Sybella asked.

"It's a month away," said Cora. "I don't even know what I'm having for breakfast tomorrow. No, I do know, because tomorrow's Thursday, and we have muesli on Thursdays. But I don't know what I'm making for the art contest."

"I've already started collecting things!" Sybella was so happy about it, she almost squeaked. "I have the best idea." It *was* the best idea too. She wanted to tell Cora, but she also wanted it to be a surprise. But a month was too long to keep a secret from one of your best friends, so she decided to tell her. "I'm making a 3D map of Aquafaba! I have thirty blue candy wrappers for the rivers, and I'm going to use those little green plastic fruit baskets you get from the farmers' market to make the mountains."

They had drawn many maps of Aquafaba in second grade and a few in third and fourth. It looked different every time because it was alive. It grew and changed. Ponds became oceans, and castles sunk to the bottom of the sea, to be raised again later when someone needed an aboveground castle for something. But they had never built it in three dimensions before. Sybella couldn't wait.

"That's so cool!" said Cora, and Sybella's heart expanded like a magical growing sponge, the kind that started as a capsule and ended up as a dinosaur. Her heart was a pteranodon.

"Do you want to help? Maybe we could enter the contest as a team!"

"Sure," said Cora. "I know where we can find materials."

"That's what I was hoping! I've been trying to think of something we can use for the beaches. We could get some real sand, but does that count as recycled if all we did was recycle it from the beach?"

"There's probably some old sandpaper in the Trash Lab," said Cora. "Maybe my dad would let us take a look. We could go back to the lab with Dani after Trash Team on Friday!"

"I can't," said Sybella. "Ms. Jackson's taking us to play a mini tournament against Roberts on Friday, remember?" She'd mentioned it to Cora a couple times. It was the Chess Club's first chance to play against another school, and Sybella's parents were taking time off work to watch.

"Oh. Right. I forgot." A gust of wind came, and Cora shivered. "I'm going inside to get my jacket. Be right back." She gave Sybella back her scarf.

"Okay." Sybella twisted the scarf in her hands, letting one end dangle over the side of the play structure. She felt something tugging on the other end of it, like a fish on a line. "Hey, what—" she started to say, but before she could finish, Marnie Stoll revealed herself, stepping out from underneath the slide with Sybella's scarf clamped in her fist.

"Can you let go? You'll mess it up, pulling on it like that."

"So what are we doing for the art contest?" said Marnie, climbing up to the platform. "We need sand? I know where there's sand."

"So do I, thanks," said Sybella. "And, um, Cora and I are already doing the contest together. I don't think you can have more than two people on the same project." She didn't think there was any rule about that, but she hoped it sounded official enough for Marnie to believe her.

"There's no rule about that," said Marnie.

Sybella thought of the very worst word she had ever heard her parents say and said it silently to herself. "Well, the deadline's passed. It's too late to sign up."

"No, it's not," said Marnie.

Sybella said the word to herself again, with more feeling.

Marnie crawled up to the platform and squashed in

next to Sybella. "I was thinking that maybe we could buy some of those foam squishy cut-outs in nature shapes, like dolphins and things, to decorate our project."

"It's not kindergarten crafts. And you have to use recycled stuff. Those foam things aren't even recyclable." Sybella wished Cora would come back.

"Yeah, but they're nature-shaped," said Marnie. "That counts."

"Pretty sure it doesn't," said Sybella. "And we're already working on our project, Marnie. You can't join our group. Sorry," she added, even though she wasn't.

Marnie was quiet for a minute, which was probably a record for her. Then she climbed back down the structure and went over to the fence by the street. Sybella watched her kicking at the trash and leaves that had accumulated next to the fence. Then she bent over the fence and reached into a pile of leaves on the other side. She unearthed a boot, held it up, made a face, and tossed it into the street. Then she sat on a swing by herself, and Sybella turned away.

A few minutes later, Sybella saw Cora coming back with her jacket, but the bell rang, and they lined up to go back inside. She wanted to tell her what Marnie had said, but there was no opportunity. Their lines separated, Cora's class heading for the library and Sybella's going back to their classroom.

Mr. Sheehy spent the afternoon showing them pictures of California native plants on the smart board and then pictures of invasive plants that were trying to take over because they grew too fast, or they didn't need a lot of water, or no animals liked to eat them. The invasive ones were like the criminals of the plant world. They did whatever they wanted to, and no one could stop them.

Sybella thought about her art project and wondered if Aquafaba had any invasive plants in it. *Probably not,* she decided as she organized her pencil case and her binder, waiting for Mr. Sheehy to call for her group to line up to go home. It wasn't a world with any bad guys, whether they were plants, animals, or anything else.

She unzipped her pencil case to put her favorite bendy pencil inside and saw a folded piece of paper that hadn't been there before. Maybe Cora had sneaked a note into her pencil case that morning before they went to their separate classes?

Putting her hands in her lap, she unfolded the note.

It was from Cora. Sybella recognized her handwriting and smiled. When had Cora had the time to sneak a note into her pencil case? Maybe that morning. Or maybe that's what she'd really been doing when she said she had to go inside at recess.

She'd made an acrostic poem for Sybella. They had

made lots of acrostics in third grade, using the first letters of their names to make a poem-y list of words about who they were and what they liked.

Cora had written her silly notes before, but she'd never sneaked them into Sybella's pencil case. Maybe there was something extra special about this one. Sybella read down the letters of her name, excited to see what Cora had written.

S
Y
Best friend
E
L
L
Abandoner

Abandoner. She shivered, as if the playground wind had blown straight through the walls.

Best friend abandoner.

What did that mean? When had Sybella ever abandoned Cora? They'd never even had a fight. And why would Cora choose a poem to say something so personal and awful to Sybella instead of saying it to her face?

When Mr. Sheehy told her group to get their jackets and backpacks, Sybella still felt cold and stiff. Her senses were jumbled. She reached for the wrong jacket, dropped it on the floor, bent to pick it up, and her head throbbed. She pulled her own jacket off its hook, snatched her backpack, and stood in line.

Why?

She thought back to recess, when she and Cora had talked about the art project, and tried to remember Cora's words, her movements, her face. Other kids sometimes said they didn't understand Cora, but Sybella did. She would have noticed if something was wrong.

There had been a lot of times at the beginning of fifth grade when Cora had zoned out, or forgotten things, or walked around under her own little cloud of gray. She'd always seemed a little worse on the days after she talked to her mom, because that's when she couldn't pretend that her mom was just out somewhere, doing errands or working, and not halfway around the world. But eventually she'd gotten used to the idea that her parents had split up, and her mom was gone for the year. She'd cheered up, and Sybella had done her best to keep her that way. They texted jokes to each other sometimes, and Sybella had even checked out a joke book from the library and picked jokes to text Cora if she thought Cora was starting to sink.

She wondered for half a second if the note was from

someone else. Maybe someone had studied Cora's handwriting and reproduced it perfectly as a prank. But the note wasn't just in Cora's handwriting, it was written on the Sustainable Fisheries notebook paper her dad had brought her from a conference, and the letters were written in the thick gray lines of the twig pencil she'd bought at the Ecology Fair last summer. They'd played Hangman dozens of times with that pencil.

The only other person who could have used that pencil, and that paper, and who might know what Cora's handwriting looked like was Kyle. But Kyle would never do that. Kyle would probably give up washing dogs for a year before he would prank Cora and Sybella. Kyle wouldn't see a chance to prank someone if it licked him on the cheek.

Was it about the mini chess tournament? Cora wasn't that petty, to accuse Sybella of *abandoning* her because she had another activity to do for one day out of the year. Was she?

Sybella's mother always talked about "clearing the air" and how you couldn't let bad feelings simmer and smoke, getting the air all dirty and making the right course impossible to see. Sybella knew she had to talk to Cora, as hard as it would be. She had to get the problem out in the open, clear the air, and then, she knew, they would be able to see each other clearly again.

Mr. Sheehy opened the door, and the kids spilled into the hallway. Sybella waited for Cora to come out of her room so they could clear the air, but when Cora finally appeared, she glanced quickly up at Sybella and said, "I have to go." And then she went.

Cora

What Happened

DR. CLARE WILSON'S VOICEMAIL

Twin Phone

"The imaginary underwater kingdom of Aquafaba regrets to inform you that it doesn't exist. Maybe it never did. If you ever went there, maybe you were really somewhere else. You thought you were in paradise, but you weren't. There are no dogs. Or waffles. And if you have a friend who lived there, they don't live there anymore, either. We don't know where they are, though. Maybe they are just lost."

Speaker Call Back Delete

Aquafaba had been invaded.

No, not invaded: betrayed. An imaginary kingdom, it turned out, was no match for the weapons of the real world.

After Cora ran from Sybella that day in the hallway, it was hard not to run again the next day, and the next. And when Kyle said to her, while she was hiding in the geography section in the school library, "What's going on? Why are you avoiding Sybella? I think she's really upset," Cora ran again.

How upset could Sybella be if she was busy making friends with Marnie Stoll? A week after Sybella had found the poem, Cora was in the nurse's office, and from the window she could see them on the playground, sitting together on top of the bars. Marnie was laughing. Cora couldn't see Sybella's face, but she imagined her smiling at whatever Marnie was saying.

She didn't blame Sybella, not really. Maybe Marnie would be a better, more loyal friend than Cora had been. Because Cora, former Aquafabian and current outcast, had been a traitor.

It was too bad that *treachery* wasn't one of Ms. Nuñez's words for the year, like *self-direction*. Because Cora was doing very well at treachery. In fact, somehow, it had been happening all along, even though she'd thought Sybella would never find out.

Her moment of treachery had happened back in September. The Trash Team had met a few times, and once, after Sybella's mom came early to pick her up, Cora had hung around while Dani put away the supplies.

As a midday treat for herself, Cora had brought some of the Belgian chocolates her mother had sent them recently. She'd put a few into her banana sandwich, and now she took the last one from her lunchbox and offered it to Dani. "My mom said I'd like Belgium. She said they put chocolate on their toast in the morning."

"For me?" Cora nodded, and Dani took the little shell. "I bet you miss your mom, don't you?"

Cora found she couldn't speak, so she nodded again, squeezing her eyes to keep the tears in.

Dani saw and understood. "Come on, let's go for a walk. We have a little while before your dad's coming to pick you up, right? Let's go get coffee. I mean, I'll get coffee, and you get whatever kids get."

"Okay." Cora sniffed again. "Kids get large decaf chai lattes with whipped cream and blueberry bagels with strawberry cream cheese."

"Kids are scammers," said Dani, smiling, but she ordered exactly that drink and bagel when they got to a café around the corner from school.

Cora had never been in this café before. It was the opposite direction from her house and the way they always went home. Square spray-painted canvases with pieces of metal and fabric glued to them hung on the walls.

"A friend of mine did all these," said Dani. "This is her show."

"I like them," said Cora. "They're kind of recycle-y."

Dani laughed. "Yeah, they are. Too bad she's not in elementary school, or she could enter them in the art contest."

Cora stood in front of a blue canvas that had an L-shaped piece of copper pipe in the middle of it. She read the little tag: *Water.* "Is it called *Water* because it's blue? Or because water goes through pipes?"

"I don't know," said Dani. "Sometimes the title is the part that makes you think the most."

They took their drinks to go in two travel mugs that Dani had brought from her truck. "I guess I've worked with your dad for long enough. I have like ten of these things. You can't recycle those to-go cups because of the plastic liner."

Cora knew that already. She knew it all, but she liked hearing it from Dani, who made everything less boring just because she wasn't boring. Cora scooped up her whipped cream with her tongue and sipped her drink happily as they walked back to school.

"So this might sound weird," said Dani, "but have you tried writing poetry? To get your feelings out? Sometimes it helps. That's what I did when I was a kid."

"I don't have feelings," said Cora, which was 100 percent completely the opposite of true. If anything, she had too many feelings. Or just *too much* feeling. Sometimes she didn't know what to do with it all. It was hard to talk about it with anyone, she knew that much.

"*Okay*," said Dani. "But let's say you *did* have feelings, like about your mom, maybe writing poems would be a good way to deal with them."

"I guess?"

Dani gave her a friendly shoulder bump. "Just give it a try."

That evening at home, Cora lay on her bed and tried writing poetry, she really tried, but all she could think of were the kind of poems she had written in third grade, using the letters of her name:

Cool
Orange
Recycling
Animals

That kind of poem was supposed to say something about her as a person, but Cora couldn't even do that. She tried one about Kyle:

Kool
Yellow
Little
Elephants

"Ugh."

Maybe the problem was that it was the wrong kind of poetry. It didn't help her get her feelings about her mom out at all. She texted Sybella to see if she wanted to come over, but Sybella was busy going to a play with her mom. Cora didn't even want to see a play, but she felt a creeping jealous tide rising up inside her.

Sybella got to see her mom every morning before school and every evening after work. Sybella's mom tucked her in at night and made her breakfast in the morning. When Cora had texted last weekend to see if she wanted to come over and feed food scraps to the worm box, Sybella had been out to brunch with her mom. And now she was out seeing a play with her mom. If she was a real friend, wouldn't she stay at home? Wouldn't she be there when Cora needed her?

She started another poem as the tide rose and rose.

S
Y
Best friend
E
L
L
Abandoner

Cora looked at what she had written and dropped her pencil. That wasn't how she felt about Sybella.

Was it?

Of course not.

She wanted to apologize to Sybella, even though Sybella had no idea what she had written. She wanted to call her mom, but in Belgium it was two in the morning and her mom would be asleep. She tried Auntie Lake, but there was no answer. She wished she could call Dani, but she didn't have her number.

Writing poetry was supposed to help her with her feelings, not mix them all up and make them worse.

Maybe it only worked if you wrote good poetry. Cora didn't think she'd ever be good enough for that. She thought about tearing the paper out of her notebook and feeding it to the worms, but she didn't want to make the worms sick.

She decided to try her mom's number anyway but hung up. Then she dialed again, and when the voicemail message came on, she knew what she needed to say. She couldn't talk directly to her mom, but she could announce her feelings for Dr. Wilson to hear later.

"May we have your attention, please. This is a public service announcement to let you know that we miss you. We understand that what you're doing is for the good of science, but we still miss you and we can't wait until you come home. Wherever that is. Thank you for listening to this important announcement."

Hanging up, Cora grabbed her notebook by one corner and tossed it across her room, as if she were too afraid of what she'd written to touch the paper it was written on.

That was September. It wouldn't have been important at all, except for one thing.

The next morning, she picked the notebook up and put it in her backpack with all her other school supplies. She'd forgotten about the disastrous attempt at writing poetry—Kyle had cheered her up by trying to do handstands against the living room wall, plus there had been blueberry millet muffins at breakfast—and she didn't think about the notebook again until Ms. Nuñez told everyone to get ready for writing workshop. Then, almost as if she'd wished it away, it wasn't there.

Maybe Kyle had borrowed it. But Kyle was in a different class, and when she asked him at recess if he'd taken it out of her backpack before school, he said, "Nope," and cartwheeled into the middle of a kickball game. When she shyly and haltingly asked Sybella if she had, just maybe, probably not, but *maybe* she'd seen Cora's notebook, Sybella said, "Uh-uh," and asked Cora to come play backward Hopscotch.

So where was it? Had she forgotten to zip her backpack up? Had the notebook fallen out on her way to school? Had it vaporized?

She really, *really* hoped it had vaporized.

And maybe it had. Maybe for once the laws of garbage had worked in her favor, and the thing she wanted to get rid of had disappeared forever. The notebook didn't turn up anywhere at school, at home, or in the gutter on the route she walked to school, and after a couple of weeks she forgot about it.

Then in March, she and Sybella talked about the art contest at recess. Cora was glad Sybella had an idea, because she had nothing. And Sybella's ideas were always good. Cora offered to get some of the materials, and she was excited about working on it together. A 3D map of Aquafaba wouldn't mean anything to anyone else, but it would mean everything to them.

When she went in to get her jacket, she saw Kyle in the library and stopped in to ask him if he wanted to do the project with them. He'd been talking about doing a collage—something with dogs, of course—but this was so much better than dogs.

"But you should see this terrier at the Humane Society," said Kyle. "Sometimes he wears a sweater!"

That meant Kyle was definitely going to do something with dogs. Cora left the library and nearly crashed into Marnie Stoll, who was running, not walking, in the hallway.

"Oh!" Marnie said. "Sorry."

"That's okay," said Cora, stepping out of Marnie's way.

"No, I mean, I'm *sorry,*" said Marnie. "You must feel so bad!"

"Why?"

Marnie bit her lip. "I would feel bad if my best friend found a mean thing I wrote about her. I would feel like a big old nope. But that's me. I think it's important to be nice to my friends."

Something mean? When had Cora ever written

anything mean about Sybella? She would never—and then it came back to her. The poem. The lost notebook.

"I was just talking to Sybella, you know, trying to help her calm down," said Marnie. "She's pretty mad."

Sybella had found the poem? Just now? Or in September? But if she'd found it in September, why hadn't she said anything then? Why be mad now? Cora's head ached as thoughts shoved and jostled around inside.

"When—what—why—" she began. "How—"

Marnie patted her shoulder. "I *know,*" she said. "It's so awful. She says she doesn't want to be your friend anymore. She said the next time she sees you, she's going to tell you exactly what she thinks of you. It's so *sad.* I thought you were *best friends.*" She let out a little squeak, like a giggle being squished by a hiccup, and skipped away.

Best friends.

Best friend abandoner.

It wasn't the worst thing you could ever think about someone—was it?—but it was the worst thing she'd ever thought about Sybella. And she hadn't even really thought it. It had dripped out of that stupid twig pencil like sap, leaving its sticky marks across the page.

Cora should have been able to explain that it was meaningless. She should have been able to say that she had been jealous and angry for thirty seconds, but then, instead of erasing the poem or tearing out that page and burying it in the worm box, she had lost track of it. The signal had dropped. The red line on the map had disappeared.

Best friend abandoner.

It wasn't just untrue, it was as far away from true as you could get. It was the Belgium of things that weren't true, as far away as you could be from truth. Sybella had never abandoned her.

The truth was, Sybella had tried harder than anyone to make Cora feel better, to distract her from her problems and help her get through this year. So what if she ate brunch with her mom? Cora would have eaten brunch with her mom if she'd been around. So what if they did things like moms and daughters were supposed to? Sybella deserved her mom, and Cora deserved nothing.

When was the last time she'd unburied herself from her own trash pile of feelings to look around and see if Sybella needed anything?

She hadn't.

She hadn't been the worst friend, but she knew she hadn't been the best friend, either.

That was the most awful thing. Not just that Sybella had found the poem, or that Sybella was angry and didn't want to be Cora's friend, but that the words themselves might be true—not for Sybella, but for Cora. She'd let her own bad feelings overflow like a landfill. It had taken a long time, as it often did, but finally the toxins had leached into the waters underground and poisoned everything.

Sybella

What Happened Next

"I feel so *sorry* for you," said Marnie, swinging her legs over the edge of the playground bars. "Cora was *so mean,* wasn't she? I mean, *yuck.*"

Sybella's cheeks warmed. "Yeah, can we stop talking about that?" She'd given up on trying to keep Marnie away. Marnie was the fly that buzzed around the room, landing on your arm and jumping away when you tried to squash it. Now, one long, awkward week after the poem had appeared in Sybella's pencil case, Marnie buzzed and Sybella simply tried to ignore her.

"Oh, sure, of course, I'm sorry. I'll stop talking about it. I mean, who even knows why she said it? She needs to explain herself. All she said to me was that she never thought you were a very good friend anyway and that—"

"Stop. Talking. About. It!" Sybella jumped down from the structure, hoping Marnie wouldn't follow her.

Cora hadn't said anything to her all week. Sybella had tried once more to clear the air, but that was looking impossible. It wasn't air anymore. It was fog. Or smog. It hovered between them, and whenever Sybella tried to open her mouth, she found she couldn't breathe properly.

Now, hoping to get away from Marnie, she went to the library to talk to Ms. Jackson about improving her opening moves for the next mini tournament, but Ms. Jackson wasn't there. Kyle was, though. He was sitting at a low table, cleaning a stack of picture books with a disinfectant wipe. How was Kyle so *good* all the time?

She hadn't talked to him all week, either. They hadn't been avoiding each other, but Sybella hadn't been trying to talk to him. And she wasn't sure she wanted to talk to him now. He probably wouldn't take sides, but Sybella didn't want to find out.

"Oh, sorry, I'll just—" she began.

"Hey, wait," said Kyle. "Can I ask you something?"

"Um, sure."

Kyle waved his wipe at the chair across from him, and Sybella sat down. She'd seen part of a movie once where a guy was in a bar and he poured out all his troubles to the bartender, who was wiping down the bar late at night after everyone else left. Kyle could be that bartender, serving up Shirley Temples and smoothies and hot chocolate to troubled fifth graders. She wanted to pour all her troubles out to him, but it was all so awkward.

"I don't know what's going on with you guys, but Cora's miserable," he said. "More miserable than normal."

"Me too." She propped her elbows on the table and rested her chin in her hands.

"Can I get you something to drink?"

"What?"

"I have half a strawberry-kiwi juice left from my lunch. You want some?"

Sybella nodded. "Thanks."

He got a paper cup from the water cooler and poured some of his juice into it for Sybella. It was like a little piece of the old magic, and she tried to smile.

"I think she hates me," Sybella said when he set the cup in front of her. "She thinks I abandoned her or something, and she won't talk to me. And I want to talk to her, but I don't. It's too confusing. Like, did I do something wrong? I don't think I did. It just happened, like we were friends one second and then we weren't."

Kyle wiped another book. "She won't talk to me

about it, either. But she's not mad. She's . . . sad." He poured the last of his juice into the little cup.

"Last call?" said Sybella, because that's what the guy with all the troubles had said in the movie.

But Kyle didn't get the reference. He said, "You *should* call her! Or text. If she saw it was you, she'd answer, I know she would. It's my day with the Twin Phone, but I'll let her have it."

"You think so?" Part of her wanted to call, because she wanted to make everything right between them, even though she had no idea what was wrong. But there was another part of her that wanted Cora to call her. Even though Marnie was never, ever right about anything, *ever,* Sybella wanted Cora to explain herself.

"Yeah," said Kyle. "Definitely. Maybe you should wait until we're at home, in case she wants some privacy. Try between five-thirty-three and five-forty-five. That's after we get off the bus and before we have to look through the neighbors' garbage." Only Kyle could make that sentence sound reasonable.

He sounded so sure, so optimistic. Sybella wanted to believe him. "Okay," she said. "I will."

At home that afternoon, Sybella rearranged her room nervously. She was only going to text Cora, but for some reason tidying her room made her feel calmer.

Sybella pushed all the materials she'd been collecting

for her art project into a corner of her room and vacuumed her rug. She brought a bag of veggie chips into her room for sustenance and was fluffing up her beanbag chair at 5:32 when her phone beeped.

It was the generic text blip, not Cora and Kyle's sea lion bark. She swiped the screen, and the text came up.

Its Marnie

"How did you get my number?" Sybella muttered, then she texted back, I'm busy, sorry

Me too

"Then why are you texting me?" But instead she wrote, Okay, see you tomorrow

5:33. She opened the conversation she had with Cora. The last text, sent over a week ago, said, Orange you glad I didn't say banana. Sybella wondered if she should start with a knock-knock joke. As if nothing had happened.

Blip. Are you still busy 🤨

Ugh. Yes

Blip. Me too 😜 I really have to go, I'm working on a project

There was no answer, and the time turned to 5:34. Sybella practiced her text aloud. "*Knock knock.* No, that's dumb. *Hey, Cora!* No. *Kyle said I should text you.* Double no. Why is this so hard?" She took a handful of veggie chips and flopped onto her beanbag chair to think.

5:37.

She took a deep breath and let it out. "You got this, Sy," she coached herself, even though she definitely did not.

5:38.

She swiped the screen again, tapped on Cora/Kyle, and typed, Knock knock, who's there, can we talk

5:39.

Bark. Can we talk who

Sybella took a deep breath again, this time in relief. Cora had answered.

Can we talk about what's going on because I don't know what happened

Blip. Are you working on our art project because I have some ideas for that

"No!" Sybella muttered, and she typed, No

Bark. I don't know what happened wither

Bark. Either

Blip. What if we use kinetic sand the kind that lives on its own 😜

Blip. Moves on its own 😜

"Stop. Texting. Me," Sybella said, making a mad face at her phone. I'll talk to you tomorrow Marnie

To Cora, she texted, Maybe we could talk about it

Bark. Okay

Blip. Or glitter like glitter sand 😂

I said I'll talk to you tomorrow Marnie

Bark. Marnie?

"No. No!" Cora. I mean you. Cora.

No answer.

No answer.

No answer.

Blip. This is gonna be the best pepper EVA 

Blip. Project 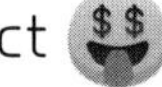

Blip. Best project EVA

Blip.

Cora

After

DR. CLARE WILSON'S VOICEMAIL

Twin Phone

"Public service announcements are supposed to be useful. But this one is a mystery. We don't know exactly what to say. That is, we know what we should say, but we don't know how to say it. Can you say things without words? If you think it's possible, please get in touch with our office, and we'll respond to your comment without any words."

Speaker
Call Back
Delete

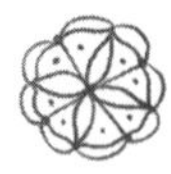

The day after the Trashlympics, instead of thinking about her art project, Cora read Penny Ellen's diary again. It was just as confusing as the last time she'd read it, and just as sad.

Oh, Lulu.

Cora read that over and over and wondered where Lulu was too. Penny Ellen had said Lulu would never save the earth, but more than forty years had gone by since then. Maybe by now she had saved it, or at least her little part of it, wherever that was.

That evening, Cora and Kyle walked to the dog park with Dr. Davis and his trash grippers. He'd said they were going there to clean up the park, but Cora knew it was mostly so Kyle could be around dogs for a while.

As they walked, Cora asked, "What's a cigarillo?"

The translator in Dr. Davis's brain that turned every question into a question about trash replied, "It's a small cigar. Cigarillos don't have built-in filters like cigarettes do, although people often smoke them through plastic filters, which they then discard on the sidewalk. There, for example." He extended the trash grippers and lifted up a whitish piece of plastic that looked like a tiny whistle. "The cigarette filter, what you see lying on the sidewalk there, and there, and over there, is the most common piece of trash across the world, and it's not biodegradable. It is, in fact, quite a health hazard."

The plastic filter went in the bag.

At the dog park, Kyle happily let dogs sniff him, and he even recognized one that had been adopted recently from the Humane Society. "Flapjack! Here, boy!"

Flapjack, a tiny Dachshund, bounded up to Kyle and put his paws on Kyle's leg. "Flapjack, this is Cora."

"Hey, Flapjack," said Cora. She watched Kyle and Flapjack play. Kyle was filled with so much love, and he was finding places for it to go. Was that what made everything look so easy for him? Cora was filled with love too, but where Kyle's was soft, hers seemed to be spiky, like Penny Ellen's. Hers hurt. It made everything harder.

They walked back home with Kyle talking nonstop

about all the cute things Flapjack had done when he was at the Humane Society. Then he started talking about Sir Walter Dog and said, "I'm going to finish my art project!" as soon as they got home.

Cora went to her room and read the art contest flyer again.

Upcycle Your Trash: It's Not Just Trash, It's Art!

The rules stated that the art had to be made of 100 percent recycled, reused, or found material, and it couldn't take up more than four square feet on a table.

She looked skeptically at the pictures of the exciting trash-related prizes: a bag of red worms for your worm box, compost thermometers, bracelets and coasters made out of recycled and compressed denim, and jump ropes made from recycled plastic bags woven together. The jump ropes looked like fun, and the bracelet was nice. She had plenty of worms in her worm box already.

Cora hadn't stayed for the awarding of the trash points at the Trashlympics because she'd been too busy hiding in the locker room and reading Penny Ellen's diary, but she knew she was nowhere near winning. She probably didn't even have a single official trash point—not that she was counting.

Kyle and Sybella were probably both contenders, though. If Cora had to place a bet, she would bet on Kyle. She'd watched him carefully piecing together his collage of Sir Walter Dog, cutting tiny squares out of cat litter bags he'd brought home from the Humane Society and sorting them by color. He'd even tested three different kinds of glue to see which worked best with the textured plastic. Sir Walter had a jaunty little green vest on, and he was posing against a backdrop of mountains and blue sky.

"I would have used dog food bags," Kyle had said while he was collecting his materials, "but there's no such thing as Fresh Scent dog food."

"You're making a dog out of cats," Cora observed, and Kyle gave a wide smile.

"I am! I bet Sir Walter would like that."

"Do you think Dad's going to let you get a dog?"

"No." The smile shrank a little, but it didn't take long for Kyle to see the bright side. "I'll just have to work harder. Maybe if I win the contest, Dad will talk to the landlady and get her to change her mind."

Now Sir Walter Dog was almost complete, and Cora was trying to draw a mustache on a paper towel tube. She'd waited a long time to get the tube, since no one in the Davis household was allowed to use paper towels instead of cotton rags unless they really, really needed them. Eventually, she'd unwound the whole roll, leaving the paper towels in a pile on the kitchen counter.

"What are you working on?" asked Kyle.

"Tube Guy," said Cora, showing off Tube Guy's beady eyes and the scraggly marker lines of his hair. "What do you think?"

"It's really . . . round!"

"Ugh." Cora dropped Tube Guy onto her desk. "I know. It's so bad. I wish Dad wasn't making me do this contest. But I don't know what to do. Tell me what to do."

Kyle picked up Tube Guy and pretended to straighten his hair. "You know what Juniper said? He said art brings people closer together. So maybe that's what you should think about. Think of something that will bring people closer together."

Sir Walter Dog, Collage #1 could do that. It would bring together people who liked collages and people who liked dogs. And people who liked Kyle. Everyone liked Kyle.

If she was being honest, as honest as Penny Ellen had been, there were only two people she wanted to bring closer to her. One of them was in Belgium, and the other one might as well have been on the moon.

Kyle set Tube Guy down gently, and Cora tipped him over and rolled him across the top of her desk. That made her think about *Water,* the piece of art she'd seen at the café with Dani. She remembered the skinny piece of copper pipe and the blue canvas and the simple name, and how sometimes a piece didn't look like much and it was the title that made you think the most.

So she thought, and a new idea came to her. She wrote her title card before she started her project. One word, in letters as neat and straight as she could make them: *Aquafaba.*

She didn't need many supplies, but what she needed had to be just right.

The night before the art contest, Dr. Davis made pizza. The dough was too thick in some places and too thin in others, but it was still pizza, piled high with cheese, veggies, and chickpeas, and Cora took a second piece, and a third, and made extra-noisy noises as she slurped her home-brewed root beer through her pasta straw.

Dr. Davis had looked at her with his scientist's face when she asked for chickpeas on the pizza. His scientist's face was basically one big question mark: "Why? Why is this happening? Why is there climate change? Why is there sewage in the oceans? Why would you ask for chickpeas on your pizza?"

"I don't have time to soak dried chickpeas," he'd said. "They'll have to come out of a can." They did have some canned and packaged goods in a cabinet, along with some bottled water and other earthquake supplies. "We should probably check the expiration dates on the food, though. It might be time to replace it anyway."

"I'll check," Cora had said. She'd taken a can out of the cabinet and checked the date (six months away, close enough), hooked the can opener to its edge, and turned the handle carefully so the edge didn't get too jagged. She'd poured off the liquid into a container and put it in the fridge with a label that said *Cora's art project, very important, do not touch*. Instead of rinsing the can and putting it in the blue bin, where all cans went, she'd put it on her desk, next to the tag she had made. It was no longer just trash. It was art.

Now they were sitting around the table, chewing thoughtfully. "The fun continues," said Dr. Davis, stretching out his legs. "How are you feeling about tomorrow's art contest?"

"Fantastic," said Kyle. Of course he was. His collage was incredible. *Sir Walter Dog, Collage #1* watched over their dinner from its place on the wall, where Kyle had hung it temporarily to take pictures to send to Dr. Wilson. "And it smells great too."

"I can see you've put a lot of thought and effort into your work," said Dr. Davis.

"Can we get a real dog?" asked Kyle. "I'll put a lot of thought and effort into it."

He looked so eager, and for once Dr. Davis didn't have a quick reply. After a minute he said, "I don't know why Lake gave you that gift certificate. She knows we can't have pets. I'm sorry, Kyle."

"That's okay," said Kyle quickly. "I knew it already.

It's fine." But he didn't look fine, and even Sir Walter Dog, when Cora looked at him again, seemed a little disappointed.

Dr. Davis rubbed his forehead, and Cora braced for the questions about her project. At least now she could say she was almost done with it, but she didn't want to have to show it to her dad. She didn't want to have to explain it to him.

She had put a lot of thought into it, but only a little effort, unless you counted weeks of agony. Ms. Nuñez had repeated several times that it was important not just to make something cute, but to say something with your art. Cora knew what she wanted her piece to say and who she wanted to say it to. She hoped the message was loud and clear.

But Dr. Davis only said, "Let's clear the table and check your trash cans. Then you can pack to go to Auntie Lake's after the contest tomorrow."

They cleaned up and checked their trash cans. Cora's was empty, but Kyle's was full of extra pieces of cat litter bags that he hadn't used in the collage. "You win!" he said to Cora.

"I win at garbage," she said. But winning at garbage was different from winning at life.

Cora

After

DR. CLARE WILSON'S VOICEMAIL

Twin Phone

"Please stay tuned for this very important—"

"Cora, she's trying to call back. Answer it!"

"Oh! Mom, you're there!"

Speaker   Call Back   Delete

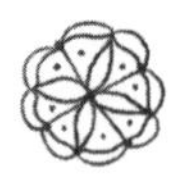

The next day, Cora was back on the university campus, not in the gym, but in a large room that had been transformed into a student art gallery. Two adults Cora didn't know were standing in front of *Sir Walter Dog, Collage #1: Mixed Media (But Mostly Cat Litter Bags).*

"Whimsical," one of them was saying. "And yet, there's a certain vulnerability you don't often see in dogs."

Or on cat litter bags, thought Cora.

Sir Walter Dog, Collage #1 had a ribbon attached to it. Second place. The ribbon wasn't the shiny polyester kind of ribbon people used at other art shows. It was made of intricately folded newspaper, like a little work of art itself. Kyle was going around shaking people's hands, answering questions, and posing for pictures for the school website.

"Kyle did a great job," said Ms. Nuñez, coming up to Cora's table. "And your piece, Cora. Wow."

Cora waited for Ms. Nuñez to call her piece whimsical or vulnerable, but Ms. Nuñez just said again, "Wow."

Kids from all over Berkeley proudly showed off their painted and glued piles of cans, paper tubes, egg cartons, and Finnish yogurt containers. There were a lot of robots and sculptures that looked like they might be trees, or people, or giraffes. Collages were popular too, but none were as whimsical as *Sir Walter Dog, Collage #1.*

Marnie Stoll's entry also got a "wow" from Ms. Nuñez. It was called *The Dog,* and it almost looked like a dog. Marnie had cut out a dog food ad from a magazine and torn it into pieces. The pieces were taped back together, but not in exactly the same places. "It's a collage," she told Cora primly. "I think Kyle stole my idea."

"Uh," said Cora. There wasn't anything else to say to that.

Sybella was standing next to her piece, which had a larger version of the folded newspaper ribbon on it. First place. Because even though they had never succeeded at making anything great out of trash before, Sybella was always first.

Ms. Nuñez was patting Sybella on the shoulder now,

but Cora couldn't hear what she was saying. Probably, "One hundred trash points for you! No, one hundred and fifty points! Two hundred!" And Sybella would go out on the bay to gather fish data, which was fine. No one else cared about fish data, whatever that was. Not even Cora. Not really.

Sybella's piece *was* good. It deserved first place. Most of the entries were just trying to make something cute out of a bunch of trash. Sybella's piece wasn't cute at all, but she had definitely tried to say something with it. And Cora knew exactly what that was.

Sybella's piece was labeled: *No Filter. Aluminum, paper, tobacco.*

She had made red lips out of old soda cans that had been cut open and pressed flat, paper teeth in different colors, and a long, brownish, tobacco tongue. Cora wondered how Sybella had collected so many butts, since neither of her parents smoked.

"I love your statement," Ms. Nuñez was saying. "It's remarkable. Disgusting, but remarkable. No filter, because of the cigarettes—"

"Cigarillos," said Sybella.

"Cigarillos. But also, to speak without a filter. To say what's on your mind. And you have a lot on your mind, Sybella."

"I have a lot on my mind," agreed Sybella.

Cigarillos. Not just the little whistle-shaped filters, but half-smoked, gummed up, toxic cigarillos. Had she smoked them herself? Or walked all over the city in a pair of blue gloves, picking up trash from the sidewalk? All to find a way to tell Cora that she was gross, that she was trash, that her tongue was made of poison? Had Sybella put that much work into finding a way to speak her mind with no filter, and without even using any words?

Or maybe she had stashed them all last week, at the Trash-In. "No gross stuff" the rules had said. But in Cora's experience with trash, gross was a matter of opinion.

She knew from reading Penny Ellen's diary that people were capable of all kinds of garbage-related revenge plots. But it surprised and stung her to see it happening right now, in her own life, as if the horrible problems of a past that wasn't even her own were doomed to recycle themselves over and over.

Cora wanted to take her piece and leave. How stupid it seemed now. How little and pointless, next to *No Filter* and the suffocating staleness of a wad of cigarillo butts. But she couldn't move.

"What's yours supposed to be?" Marnie Stoll asked, drifting by again with her participation ribbon in her hand, not on her piece, where it was supposed to be. "It's just a chickpea can. A chickpea can with chickpea water in it."

"It is not," said Cora, close to tears. Because she was always first at that.

The card she had handwritten so carefully sat on the table next to her piece.

Cora Davis
Aquafaba
Steel, paper, BPA-free lining, aquafaba

Aquafaba (n.) 1. A viscous liquid derived from cooking or soaking legumes such as chickpeas, used as a substitute for egg whites in baking; 2. Found art; 3. An imaginary kingdom, the best place ever for the best friends ever; 4. A place that was lost.

If Sybella had come to look at Cora's piece, she would have seen the can and the card, and Cora hoped she would recognize that it was an apology. But Sybella was busy answering questions about *No Filter,* and maybe it was better that way. Sybella had already said all she needed to say.

"Maybe," said Marnie, overemphasizing her words, "you should write a *poem* about it. A-Q-A-F-A-B-A. What are you going to write about that?"

Marnie kept drifting, and Cora wondered what she'd meant. There was something behind those words, not just her bad spelling, but something bigger. *Poem.*

A picture flashed into Cora's mind. *Poem.* Her lost notebook. Marnie. Sybella.

Selfish, thoughtless Marnie. She'd managed to think of something after all.

She wanted to tell Sybella what she knew had happened, to say, "It wasn't my fault! I don't know how she did it, or why she found my notebook way back in September and hung onto it just so she could do this to us, but Marnie set us up!" Then they could be mad at Marnie instead of being mad at each other. But Sybella and her parents had already left. Marnie's mother swept in, declared the event a "raging success, Angel Puff," and dragged her daughter out behind her.

Slowly the room emptied, and Cora, Kyle, and Dr. Davis were among the few people left. Cora picked up her empty can and its card and went to look again at *Sir Walter Dog, Collage #1,* which was going to stay on display through the end of April with the other winning works of art, so that schools from all over town could see it.

"It didn't work?" said Kyle.

Cora shook her head. She'd never explained to Kyle about the poem, or her own treachery, or the message behind her art project, but somehow she thought he knew anyway, because Kyle was like that. She didn't want to confess it all, even now that she had the missing piece. Her brain felt fizzy and heavy at the same time. She just wanted to go home.

"How do you do it?" she asked Kyle.

"Do what?"

"Be so good all the time."

Kyle didn't answer, because there was no answer to that question. Kyle was what he was, just as Marnie was what she was, and Cora was what she was. "I think *you're* good," he said to Cora, and a tear fell from her cheek into *Aquafaba*.

Before they left for Sausalito, Cora planned to leave one more PSA for Dr. Wilson, but Dr. Wilson video-called the Twin Phone before Cora could leave the message.

Kyle held up his ribbon for *Sir Walter Dog, Collage #1*. "Honey!" Dr. Wilson said. "Congratulations! Is there going to be a collage number two?"

"Maybe," said Kyle. "I could use a different material. I have a lot of wool. And Cora has a loom."

"You can have my loom," said Cora.

Dr. Wilson laughed. "I have an idea," she said. "What if you had a real dog?"

"I asked Dad," said Kyle. "Mrs. Pruitt won't let us."

"I know you can't have one at Dad's place, but you can have one at mine."

"In Belgium? How would I ever pet it? Or take it for walks?"

"No, silly. At my new place. In Berkeley. I signed the lease today. I move in July first. It's got bedrooms for both of you, and dogs are allowed."

"You're coming home?" Cora and Kyle shouted at the same time, and Kyle added, "I can have a dog?" Tears ran down both their faces.

"Yes." Dr. Wilson was crying too. "Yes to both."

Cora

After All

DR. CLARE WILSON'S VOICEMAIL

Twin Phone

"We're sorry to bother you with another public service announcement. We know you just fell asleep, and we know how important a good night of sleep is for your health. You have told us that many times. But we just very much need to announce that, um, we love you. Thank you for your attention."

Speaker Call Back Delete

TWIN PHONE VOICEMAIL

Dr. Clare Wilson

"We are pleased to announce that our new headquarters will have a small yard and, naturally, full recycling capabilities. All the same rules will be in effect, with the exception of one: We will no longer accept feelings for disposal. It turns out that program wasn't working very well, and there are many more effective ways to handle feelings, although we understand that sometimes they are slippery and unpleasant. For instructions on how to deal with feelings, please refer to sections M, O, and M of your handbook."

Speaker Call Back Delete

Auntie Lake suggested making Belgian waffles again, but Cora asked if they could make a cake. She didn't have to say what they were celebrating, because she and Kyle had talked about their mom, and dogs, and art since the minute Auntie Lake had arrived to pick them up.

"A perfect idea," said Auntie Lake. She put her arms around the twins. "Things get better, don't they?"

Auntie Lake was right. Her mother was coming home.

Things wouldn't be exactly the same as they'd been before, but that was all right. She was making another home for them, where there would be a dog for Kyle and none of the arguments and sadness of their old home together. It was different, but in some ways it was better.

"Some things get better," Cora agreed. "But some things don't."

"Maybe *some things* need a little more help," said Auntie Lake.

Later on, when she was full of sugar and refined flour, and they were all bathed in the soft light of the TV and slowly disappearing into the soft cushions of Auntie Lake's sofa, Cora put her head on Auntie Lake's shoulder and said, "I'm sorry about your friend. The one who . . ." She looked up at the box of bracelets that had been made long ago for a friendship that had disappeared.

"Thank you, sweetheart," said Auntie Lake. "So am I. It happened in college. Cancer. And you know, we hadn't even talked for years before that. We got into a silly fight once, and we made up for a while, but then I moved, and we lost track of each other. It is the worst thing in this world, to lose people. And then to lose them for good."

To lose track of someone: Cora pictured Auntie Lake's friend waving from the back of a train and being sucked away into a huge, dark forest, where the tracks were invisible. Lost track.

You could try to put a trash tracking tag on a

friendship, but just because you knew where something was, it didn't mean you could keep it forever. Even a tracking tag wouldn't have saved Auntie Lake's friend from cancer. They might have had a little more time together, that was all.

"Can I look at the bracelets again?" Cora asked. "I mean, if you don't mind?"

Auntie Lake smiled. "Actually, that's a very good idea. I'd almost forgotten." She took the box off the shelf and gave it to Cora, who slid the panels, found the key, and unlocked the box.

Auntie Lake's bracelets were in a tangled pile in the box, but there was another tangled pile too.

"My friendship bracelets!" Cora gasped. "But I threw these away."

"You of all people should know that throwing something away isn't the end of the story," said Auntie Lake, and Cora hugged her so fast and so fiercely that Auntie Lake fell back against the cushions. Kyle hugged her from the other side, and together they sunk deeper into the couch. Cora might have cried if she hadn't cried so much already that day. Tears were her renewable resource, but they took time to come back.

Instead she yawned, and Auntie Lake yawned, and Kyle yawned. Yawns were contagious, like everything else, like friendship bracelets and arguments and cigarillos.

"Do you think," said Cora, yawning again, "that I could turn in my gift certificate now? For the thing I need the most?"

Sybella

After All

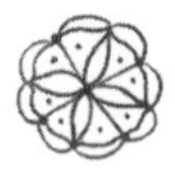

It was Sybella, this time, who was the first to cry. She cried silently out in the hall while her parents were still talking to Mr. Sheehy, because she didn't want them to see.

Cora hadn't even looked at *No Filter.* They were as lost as ever. How were you supposed to find someone once you had lost her, and if you did find her, what then?

"Art brings people closer together," Juniper had said. Sybella had tried, with her entry, to bring herself a little closer to Cora. She'd worked alone on the project because even though Marnie had wormed her way onto Sybella's team for the Trashlympics, there was no way Sybella was doing the art project with her.

She dropped the idea of the Aquafaba map, although

now that she thought about it, it would have made a more obvious statement. But she'd gotten carried away with the idea that she could say something with her art, and what better way to say something than with a mouth?

She had made a smiling mouth, because, even after their fight, it made her happy to be friends with Cora. *No Filter,* because she was not telling lies. And a tongue made of cigarillos, gathered from the local dog park—who knew so many people with dogs smoked?—because it was a code, her way of saying to Cora what Penny Ellen had tried to say to Lulu: *Find me.*

But maybe Cora didn't know the code. The half of the diary that Cora had might not say anything about cigarillos. Or maybe she hadn't even read it. Sybella wished she'd chosen something else that Cora would have recognized. Brussels sprouts? Alcatraz wrappers? But maybe leaving a trail, a clue, wouldn't have worked, no matter what she used. It hadn't worked for Penny Ellen, had it? It didn't look like Lulu had found her.

On the way out to the car, Sybella's dad tried to swing her in a circle like he had when she was little, but they ended up doing an awkward ring-around-the-rosy dance instead. Her mom said, "I'm so proud of you, Sy!" for the sixth time.

"You said that already, Mom." Sybella let go of her dad's hands.

"I'm going to keep saying it too, because it's true. And when something's true, you can say it as many times as you want."

You can say it, Sybella thought, *but if no one's going to listen, does it matter?*

"Speaking of saying something," said her mom, "did you see Cora's piece?"

Sybella sighed. "No." She hadn't because she'd been busy, and also because seeing Cora's piece meant seeing Cora, and she'd been hoping to let her art do the talking for her.

"You should go back and take a look. Come on."

They went back into the gallery, searching for Cora's piece. Sybella found it next to Kyle's dog collage and read the title.

Aquafaba.

The can was . . . just a can. With a little water in it. A little bit of aquafaba, Sybella realized. She peered into the can, as if something magical might pop out of it. A little bit of Aquafaba.

She read the description Cora had written: *An imaginary kingdom, the best place ever for the best friends ever. A place that was lost.*

Was it?

Penny Ellen had lost, and Lulu had lost, but that didn't mean Sybella and Cora had to lose too.

She looked around the room for Cora, but she and Kyle were both gone. Why had Cora left this here? She could have taken it home to recycle, since it wasn't going to stay on display in the gallery. Did she think it wasn't worth saving? Or had she left it for Sybella to find, a marker on the trail back to her?

The Story of Lulu Van Allen

(not her real name)

Penny Ellen Chambord was not lost. She was Lulu's best friend, and she died too young. Not at age eleven, but still young, frozen in time at age twenty.

Lulu grew up and began to use her real name, which she had never liked as a child, because it wasn't a regular name. As a kid, she had liked the sound of Lulu, her mother's nickname for her. It was punchy, a little silly, but still strong. Lulu was a girl who could fight tigers and jump out of airplanes.

Maybe that's why she dropped it. She grew up, grew out of being a kid, and realized she wasn't going to fight tigers or jump out of airplanes. She was going to travel, she realized, and have a job, maybe get married. She was never going to have children of her own, but she would be one of those people who was always around children, starting with that funny-looking Frisby baby in Violet Dixon's neighborhood. Ratly Frisby, she called him when no one else was around, although his name was Duncan.

He grew up too, and looked less like a rodent and more like a person. Lulu went to Mathews Street and babysat for him sometimes, even after the Roadside Clean-Up Crew stopped cleaning up roads and turned into the premiere spy agency in the neighborhood and Lulu stopped being friends with Violet Dixon.

Looking back, it was the highlight of her seventh-grade career, the day she stopped being friends with Violet Dixon.

"Penny Ellen Chambord broke into my house," Violet said to Lulu at the end of a very nice week of making *Save the Earth* posters and picking up litter in the park. "She broke into your house. The least you can do is break into her house."

"Why?" said Lulu.

"If I have to tell you, you don't deserve to know," said Violet.

"I'm not a spy," Lulu said, hoping that would be the end of it. She thought about the note Penny Ellen had left with the tangled pile of friendship bracelets. She knew what it said, but the damp blob where a tear had fallen made it look like it said, "You can keep your friendship lies to yourself." She wasn't sure which was worse. She hadn't lied to anyone about Penny Ellen, exactly, but then again, she hadn't really told the truth.

"Huh," scoffed Violet. "How are you going to get anything done in this world if you don't want to get your hands dirty?"

Lulu saw, in that moment, that Violet Dixon would grow up too. And when she did, she wouldn't be a very nice person. But she just said, quietly, "I get my hands dirty all the time. I pick up litter."

Violet, who had picked up litter *and* a worm to throw on Penny Ellen's shoe, scoffed again. "Not dirty enough." It was Violet's idea to put the bag of cigarillo butts on Penny Ellen's porch. "Like a warning," she said, but she didn't say what kind of warning it was.

People who are not very nice often get their way because they are hard to say no to. Lulu found it impossible to say no to Violet, who egged her on about breaking into Penny Ellen's house. Violet wouldn't go with her, because she said someone needed to stay behind at headquarters, whatever that meant. So, one day in May, when Lulu knew Penny Ellen would be going with her mother to a potluck dinner at the Methodist church, she took Penny Ellen's key from its hiding place under the potted cactus—she had always told Penny Ellen that wasn't a safe place to keep it—and crept quietly and carefully into the Chambords' house.

Penny Ellen's diary was not under her mattress. It was in the second most obvious place: the top drawer of her desk. Next to it was Lulu's own diary, smaller, with no lock. She wondered what Penny Ellen had thought of her diary, so flagrantly stolen, full of lists of the things she was going to do to save the earth.

She put her own diary in her pocket and took out Penny Ellen's, a red leather-covered book with a little brass lock that Lulu had given her as an early birthday present. The key to the lock was on the same ring as Penny Ellen's house key. Penny Ellen really was terrible at these things.

Lulu whispered, "Mercy—have mercy on me, someone," as she put the key into the lock.

Mercy wasn't a strong enough magic word. The key, a cheap little thing that would probably have opened a hundred other red leather diaries, snapped in the lock. Lulu, possessed by the angry and vengeful spirit of Violet Dixon, who wasn't dead but who was angry and vengeful nonetheless, found Penny Ellen's sewing scissors and hacked through the strap that held the lock until the little diary fell open in her hands.

Penny Ellen's handwriting was abominable. Lulu read the first few pages, which showed that Penny Ellen was feeling angry and vengeful too. She sat on Penny

Ellen's bed to read the rest. She wouldn't steal the diary. She wouldn't go that far. Penny Ellen and her mother had been going to these potluck dinners for years, and they always lasted forever, so there was time.

Or not.

Lulu heard the front door open, followed by the sound of wheezing—Penny Ellen's mother—and arguing—Penny Ellen. "Well, if they ask you not to blow smoke directly into the macaroni and cheese, you ought to listen," said Penny Ellen. "I don't care if Mrs. Ogleby did it first."

Lulu, frozen on the bed, heard Penny Ellen stomp up the stairs and then down the hall. She would have hidden in the closet, but Penny Ellen had no closet. She would have scrambled under the bed, but Penny Ellen's bed was directly on the carpet. So she stayed frozen, holding the diary, until Penny Ellen appeared in the doorway.

"Oh," said Penny Ellen. "You found me."

"It wasn't hard," said Lulu. "I know where you live."

"I live at the end of a trail of cigarillo butts," said Penny Ellen mysteriously.

"I've been here a thousand times," said Lulu, which was probably true. "But I should go."

"Don't let me stop you," said Penny Ellen.

Lulu stood. She put the red leather diary on Penny Ellen's desk, but Penny Ellen picked it up again. "Here," she said. "Take this with you."

"I already read part of it," said Lulu.

"Then take the rest of it," said Penny Ellen. She opened the diary and pulled at the pages.

"Don't rip it!" said Lulu.

But Penny Ellen, possessed by her own angry and vengeful spirit, summoned all her strength and did the kind of thing you can only ever do once in a lifetime. She tore the binding of her diary straight down the center and handed the back half to Lulu.

"For you," she said. "The agony of victory, the thrill of defeat. Enjoy."

Lulu left Penny Ellen's house feeling like she had undergone a religious transformation, although she had been nowhere near the potluck dinner at the Methodist church. But she knew one thing: Her friendship with Penny Ellen had been a victory from the start. She wondered if Penny Ellen still wanted to be friends after all that had happened. Lulu wanted the thrill of that particular victory again, but she had some work to do first.

She told Violet that the Roadside Clean-Up Crew was finished, and she didn't want to be friends with her anymore. Violet said, "I'm turning it into a spy agency, anyway, so nuts to you."

"Don't let me stop you," said Lulu.

"You can't," said Violet Dixon.

Many years later, when Lulu was going by her real name, she saw a picture on the website of the *Washington Post*. It showed a woman glaring at the camera, under the headline "Would-Be Spy Hands over Emails, Worms to Undercover Agents."

"I'm glad she made something of herself," murmured Lulu, now going by Lake (her real name). It wasn't a regular name, but it suited her. Lake Placid, some people called her, because it was true, she was very calm.

It was funny how people's names changed sometimes. Here was Violet Dixon in the news, getting her hands dirty and going by the name Angel Charles, as if she had wished herself into an episode of that old spy show *Charlie's Angels* and gotten lost somewhere inside. And then there was Ratly Frisby, whose mother had remarried and given her son her new last name. Ratly Davis didn't sound as melodious as Ratly Frisby, but privately, that was how she always thought of him. Even after he grew up and looked less like a rat and more like the professor of garbology that he was.

It was funny too how people came into your life and took up residence there. Penny Ellen had done that, all those years ago, and Ratly Frisby and his children, Cora and Kyle, and now Dani. She and Dani had met a few months before, when she received a mysterious phone call from someone who announced, awkwardly, "You don't know me, but I know you. Penny Ellen Chambord was my great-aunt."

Dani was the one who should have been a spy, not Violet Dixon or Angel Charles or whoever she was now. Dani had found Penny Ellen's half of the diary in her Grandma Ruth's house when she was getting ready to move Ruth into a senior living condo. When Dani had asked Ruth if she remembered anything about her younger sister, Penny Ellen, and her friends or problems, Ruth had said, "Penny Ellen had nothing but friends and problems, as I recall," and went on to mutter about no-good Dixons and watery Van Allens who named their children things like River, Ocean, and Lake. With that information, Dani tracked Lake down and called her just before Christmas.

"How did you find me?" Lake had asked.

"It wasn't hard," Dani had said. "You're not that far away."

Dani had never met Penny Ellen, of course, since she'd died thirteen years before Dani was born. But she'd pieced it all together: Ruth had moved out while Penny Ellen was in third grade and never came back. But Ruth had had a baby, who grew up and had a baby, and that baby was Dani, who found Lake, all because she'd read her great-aunt's diary.

When Lake had asked why Dani wanted to find her, when Dani had never even met her great-aunt Penny Ellen, Dani had said, "Because I wanted to know the whole story."

"You have the diary," said Lake.

"Only half of it," said Dani. "I only have the first half."

"That's because I have the second half," said Lake.

Dani came over to visit Lake for the first time during winter break, and that's how they found out that they had something else in common: Ratly Frisby, although Dani agreed she would never use that name when she was working for him in the Trash Lab. And then there were Ratly Frisby's children.

"Cora reminds me of myself at that age," Dani said to Lake.

"When you get old enough, all children remind you of yourself," said Lake.

Lake let Dani read the second half of the diary, and she reread the first half. "It's funny how things fit back together," she said. "Even after all this time."

Lake (Lulu) and Penny Ellen had fit back together only for a little while, but it was a victory, anyway, in Lake's mind. It would always be a victory, even after Lulu's mother decided to move across the San Francisco

Bay to Marin, where she and Lulu lived in a swirl of fog with a persimmon tree in the front yard.

Years later, Lake thought of Penny Ellen's "agony of victory" when she heard through a friend in college that Penny Ellen, who had spent her childhood trying to save the earth from being overrun with garbage and her mother from being overrun with lung cancer, had herself died of an undiscovered brain tumor.

It was a victory, but it could have been a better one. She had lost track of Penny Ellen after the move, and maybe that didn't have to happen. Maybe she could have held on to the red line and followed it back, just once, to say goodbye.

They never had said a real goodbye.

After the Roadside Clean-Up Crew became a premier spy agency and Violet Dixon was lost to the world of intelligence, Penny Ellen Chambord and Lulu Van Allen had gone swimming and had sleepovers, and they had even argued about how many times around Earth a year's worth of disposable diapers would go.

When Lulu came to tell Penny Ellen that she was moving, Penny Ellen was standing in her yard, holding a shovel and wearing her *Not All Those Who Wander Are Lost* T-shirt.

"We're not lost," said Lulu. "Are we?"

"How can you lose something that's right in front of

you?" said Penny Ellen, throwing clods of dirt behind her from the tip of her shovel.

"Are you planting a garden?" asked Lulu.

"I'm going to live underground," said Penny Ellen. "I'll stay warm in winter and cool in summer while the rest of these suckers are wasting electricity."

"I'm going to live in Marin County," said Lulu. "I wish I could live underground."

"Well, stay cool," said Penny Ellen, who had dug a hole deep enough to put one foot in. She leaned on her shovel.

"Stay cool," said Lulu.

And Penny Ellen wandered off, still holding her shovel. Although now, thinking about it, Lake wondered if Penny Ellen had stayed put, stayed cool, and it was she, Lulu, who had wandered off.

* * *

In March of their fifth-grade year, Cora and Kyle had talked and talked about the celebration party they wanted to have at Lake's house. Lake was happy to have them over, even if it was to celebrate an imaginary world, and she was excited to meet their friend.

But when April came and Lake picked them up at the ferry dock, it was clear that something had happened. No one said a word to her about it, but no one had to.

Friendship gone cold, like a splash of icy water, did not have to be announced.

She had tried to say something to the children without using any words—she knew exactly what was in the small wooden box she had asked Sybella to open, and she had hoped that the tangle of friendship ties would jump-start a conversation between them about what had gone wrong. The girls were wearing their own bracelets, after all. Some things didn't change.

Her little plan didn't work. It was a strained weekend, and when she saw the children again later that month for their birthday, it seemed that not much had changed.

When they saw Dani that evening on their way home, Lake realized they had never told the children the funny story of Penny Ellen and Ruth, Dani and Lake, and the diary that had brought them together. There was no time then, when Kyle pulled her in one direction to talk about dogs, and Cora and Dani went in the other direction chasing after an old boot.

Later, when they'd all walked to the Davis's apartment and said goodbye, and Dani and Lake went out for coffee, Lake brought up the diary, and Dani said, "Let's not tell them. Let's show them."

They'd agreed that maybe something could be done. Maybe they were being nosy, maybe it wasn't any of their business, but neither of them wanted to stand by and watch a friendship fall apart.

"I know things change with friends," said Dani. "But maybe it doesn't have to change so fast."

"There are two lies about friendship," Lake said. "One is that it never changes, and the other is that it always has to change."

"What would you do differently with Penny Ellen, if you could go back?" asked Dani.

"I don't know," said Lake. "I have an awful feeling that I would do everything the same, because I would be the same person. That's the problem. I messed things up, even when I was trying to fix them."

They'd plotted like a couple of amateur spies. They knew they couldn't fix Cora and Sybella's problems for them, since no one can learn from experience if they haven't experienced something for themselves. But they thought they might be able to light the way for the girls, to show them that there was a way back, somewhere. The girls just had to find it.

The diary was their guide, like a set of technical instructions, an exploded diagram of how a friendship worked, and then didn't work, and then tried to work again.

"How will we do it?" asked Lake.

"I don't know yet," said Dani. "Should we ask

Ratly—*Dr. Davis*—to help us? Cora's his daughter, after all."

"Oh, no," said Lake quickly. "I haven't told him about any of this. He'd try to clean things up, but he'd only make a mess of it. Trust me."

They'd left the café, and Dani's phone had beeped. She stopped in front of one of the kids who was sitting against the wall with her knees drawn up to her chin and her feet pigeon-toed in a pair of sorry-looking black boots.

"Excuse me, can I ask you a question?" said Dani, and the girl looked up, surprised that anyone would have anything good to ask her. They talked, and Lake listened.

It turned out that the boots had belonged to Mica—that was her name—to begin with. But she had fallen asleep, and someone, just to be mean, had stolen one of them and thrown it away. And Dani had found it and put a tracker on it, but she'd lost it again. Then, out of the blue, Mica had found the boot again, by an elementary school fence, as if it had been waiting for her all along. So now she had both again.

"Some things just go together," Mica said to Dani, and Dani grinned and said, "Yeah. They do."

* * *

The Trashlympics were happening the next day, and what better opportunity was there for Lake and Dani to give new life to old things? Dani bound the two halves of the diary together with duct tape and brought the diary with her—driving all the way to Sausalito to pick up the other half from Lake's house—and she'd planned to pull Cora and Sybella aside and show it to them, telling them the story of a broken friendship from long ago. But when her bag was accidentally emptied onto the pile for Capture the Trash and Cora and Sybella had both reached for the diary, she knew that their plan, like all complicated devices, had a life of its own.

They would have to wait and hope and see what happened. Because some things do go back together.

Cora

Now

From inside the classroom of the *Alleen B,* Cora could hear small waves splashing against the hull. *"Aquafaba patria est?"* asked Cora, meaning, in this case, "Is Aquafaba your country?"

Sybella nodded.

"I'm sorry," said Cora, which she suddenly knew was what she should have said all along.

She wanted to add that somehow Marnie had made all this happen, that Marnie had found her notebook, saved the poem, and given it to Sybella as part of some plan to split them up and step into their friendship like it was her own. But she didn't. It didn't matter. Whatever Marnie had done was only possible because of what

Cora had done first. Nothing was going to change that.

"I miss Aquafaba," said Cora, still feeling shy as they sat waiting for the skipper of the *Alleen B* to tell them, probably, that they were delinquents and she was going to make them swim back to shore. "I miss . . . *you*. Do you want to go back?"

"If we can go back together," Sybella said. "We're Aquafabians. We're never not friends."

Cora's heart swelled. "I'm sorry," she said again.

"I know," said Sybella. "Me too."

They sat quietly for a moment and took in the sunlight, the waves, and the smell of fish. It was perfect, Cora realized. Perfect and very educational.

"Why did you throw the fish back?" Cora asked.

"I don't know," said Sybella. "You know that diary? I know I only got half of it, but it made me think about things. About friendship and losing people. What if those fish were lost? What if their fish friends were looking for them? I couldn't stand that. I just . . . I just love everything so much."

"I know you do," said Cora.

"I felt so sorry for Penny Ellen," said Sybella. "And I still have all these questions. Like, why did they have to fight? And what happened after all that? Maybe we could trade our halves of the diary so we can each read the whole thing?"

"Yeah," said Cora. "And then we could put them back together."

"I have duct tape," said Sybella.

"Or we could sew them together with embroidery thread," said Cora. "Like a friendship bracelet."

Sybella smiled.

Maybe if they both knew the whole story, they would have the answers. Or maybe they wouldn't. Cora still wanted to know what had happened to Penny Ellen, but for now, she had the answer she needed most.

Eventually the skipper came out. They didn't have to swim for shore or walk the plank. Their only consequence there on the *Alleen B* was that they had to promise to be better listeners, which they did, and to clean up the mess Sybella had made, which they also did.

They even collected a little fish data in the end. Cora grabbed the remaining fish, cold and slippery, from the buckets and identified them, because she had spent a long time memorizing the fish species from the posters. Sybella measured them, and then they threw the fish into the bay and watched them disappear into the dark water, where they were meant to be.

Dr. Davis was there to meet them when the *Alleen B* docked. "Well, girls, did you learn something?" he asked.

Cora had learned that marine scientists really, really did not like it when you didn't follow directions. She had learned that it was harder to rescue a fish than you might think, and that other things weren't as hard to rescue as you'd feared.

But she didn't think Dr. Davis was talking about any of those things.

So she said, "No," even though it wasn't true at all.

As they walked to the bus stop to go home, Cora looked back at the bay. The air over the water seemed to shimmer and bend.

"Can you see that?" she asked Sybella, pointing into the distance.

Sybella squinted. "Yeah. Of course," she said. "It's everywhere."

AUTHOR'S NOTE

Although *The Friendship Lie* is a work of fiction, I had to do a lot of research for the background to Cora, Kyle, and Sybella's story.

First, garbology is a real thing! An anthropologist named William Rathje wanted to study modern garbage, just like archaeologists study ancient garbage to learn about civilizations from long ago. Dr. Rathje created the Garbage Project to study human behavior through what we leave behind: our trash.

The program that Cora and Kyle's father, Dr. Davis, runs at the University of California, Berkeley, is based on a program developed at the Massachusetts Institute of Technology's Senseable City Lab. In 2009, the lab ran a program in Seattle called Trash Track using trackers based on cell phone technology to follow trash and recyclables from the drop-off point to their destination. You can see the archived web page of the project at http://senseable.mit.edu/trashtrack/index.php

The idea for the Trashlympics came from Harvard's Garbage Games (although I found the name "Trashlympics" in the Chesapeake Bay Foundation's Stream Cleanup Handbook, along with Triashlon and Trash & Field). You can see how to hold your own Capture the Trash event here: https://green.harvard.edu/tools-resources/how/garbage-games

Finally, I spent some time thinking about how I can reduce my own impact on the planet and how a family might use less, recycle more, and keep trash out of our landfills and waterways. I haven't used a pasta straw yet, but I did try a linguine coffee stirrer!

ACKNOWLEDGMENTS

Just as it takes a community working together to make a dent in our enormous problems with garbage, ocean plastic, and all the other things Dr. Davis worries about for a living, it takes a community to put a book into the world. Thanks to my indefatigable agent, Molly Ker Hawn, who deserves an armful of friendship bracelets; my editor Eliza Leahy, who skillfully tracks my words and has never once compared them to trash; the entire Capstone Trashlympics team, including Beth Brezenoff, Tracy Cummins, Alison Deering, Kay Fraser, Laura Manthe, and Hilary Wacholz; Natasha Hanova, for giving me the benefit of your experience and especially the insights into twins; Laura Hensley, for helping to sort and tag my words; Traci Post, for sorting through the final wreckage; and Ramona Kaulitzki-Kyle and Sybella would share first place in the art contest with you anytime.

On June 14, 2017, a disastrous fire broke out in London's Grenfell Tower. Through an auction led by Molly Ker Hawn and Harriet Reuter Hapgood, I auctioned the opportunity to choose a character's name in my next book. At long last, Clare Wilson gets her due. Thanks to Fiona Wilson for the contribution to Authors for Grenfell.

My uncle Barry, former skipper of the research vessel that I based the *Alleen B* on—maybe a dashing skipper will save the day in a future book? My uncle Don, who showed me the Fish House and told me that it's hard to build cabinets with no flat surfaces. Xan, who has a tattoo on the inside of her elbow and informed me that it does indeed hurt. And, always and forever, my daughters.

ABOUT THE AUTHOR

Rebecca Donnelly was born in England and grew up in California. Now she writes and recycles in a small town in northern New York and has written for *School Library Journal* and *The Horn Book*. Her debut middle-grade novel, *How to Stage a Catastrophe*, was an Indies Introduce and Kids' Indie Next List pick. *The Friendship Lie* is her second novel.

THE FRIENDSHIP LIE